CROSSINGS

SHORT STORIES

MALA NAIDOO

Naidoo, Mala

Title: *Crossings*

Print ISBN : 978-0-6455450-3-6

For my mother and daughter

ABOUT THE AUTHOR

Mala Naidoo is an Australian author. She has worked as an educator in Australia, and in South Africa during the grip of apartheid atrocities, and the early days of its dismantling. Mala Naidoo upholds *justice for all* in her novels, short stories and poems on culture, race, gender, and identity. Her writing mission is: *in our angst and joy we are ONE under the Sky of Humanity*

I shall be telling this with a sigh
Somewhere ages and ages hence...

~The Road Not Taken~
Robert Frost

SHADOWS AND LIGHT

To live in the shadows offers safety, for a while, to the detriment of the soul's light. Freedom is a prerogative gifted as birth that no human hand should enslave.

SHADOWS AND LIGHT

I crossed the border into the eastern state of my imagination. After countless failed attempts, I was dragged back, each time, kicking and screaming into a life I did not want.

MY PARENTS ENTERTAINED the notion that their best friends Seth and Lorraine would be family when their children married. Family gatherings and holidays were enjoyable as children, but I wanted another life, one that bore no resemblance to my growing-up years.

Ritchie was a friend, nurtured from the cradle by Lorraine and Seth and my parents. How many parents does a kid need? My parents were overpowering in every way. Ritchie was sweet on me from our teenage days, but he was not my type. Much too docile, too submissive, and compliant. He caved to his parent's every whim and I might add command.

At sixteen I left home without telling my parents. I went to my friend Amy's family farm. She was a border at our school. I admired her confidence, and her ability to be comfortable with who she was. We struck up a loyal friendship, and when I needed space, she invited me over telling her mother my parents were travelling overseas, and I would be spending the summer with them. Her family were laid-back, never asking questions, or enforcing expectations upon their children. What a life!

I slept a blissful two nights with Amy's family, riding horses by day, enjoying a barbecued dinner, and chatting long into the night under a starry sky. It was an exhilarating feeling doing what made me happy. My parents tracked me down after calling every parent in my year group. Amy's mother apologised for not checking with my parents if it was acceptable for me to spend the summer with them. That's the type of family Amy had. They trusted each other and allowed her to take control of her friendships and most of what she did. I ran a mile from everything my parents wanted me to do! I tried to. Unsuccessfully.

I lived with the constant command, 'No, you can't, Sasha!' or 'What decent young woman does that?' I was just never good enough. Do you blame me for my rebellious attitude, when I was not allowed to think for myself, let alone act on anything I wanted to do?

The homecoming after my brief getaway at Amy's home was dinner with Ritchie and his family. That was the end of my school days. My mother home-schooled me after what she called my ungrateful behaviour. Homeschooling was deemed a way to prevent a recurrence of my belligerent ways.

I hated weekly dinners with Richie and his parents. I

hated being home-schooled even more. All I ever learned was how one should be a good, grateful daughter and wife.

Ritchie and I were constantly thrown together, and I heard, ad nauseam, what a lovely couple we would be. 'Would be,' was all I could stomach until that fateful day when Ritchie's mother, Lorraine, died in a car accident. Seth was driving when he fell asleep at the wheel on a trip back from his parent's wedding anniversary party. Nobody paid much attention to how Ritchie, asleep in the back seat, sustained no injuries. His mother died instantly when their car hit a tree.

My parents fell apart when Lorraine died, and I felt the pressure to support Ritchie through his grief. I desired to be carefree, but guilt surfaced if I turned away from comforting Ritchie. Guilt was conditioned from the cradle. All I was prepared to offer was a listening ear and company. I was eighteen when Lorraine passed. Ritchie turned nineteen that year.

When Seth suggested we marry while we were in college, I ran off with another fellow who showed casual interest in me. I had no feelings for him, but he was my ticket out of a marriage I did not want. What a choice!

I was on the road with Guy, an emerging stand-up comedian, for almost six months, until one night a brawl broke out at the pub where he performed. I left Guy that night not wanting an unsettled, violent life, not knowing when he would have the next gig.

I took a job at a casino in Garryville, far north of my hometown. My parents abhorred gambling so that made me feel safe from ever being found.

One unexpected night while I was at my roulette table, a woman sidled up to me at my workstation. She got close enough to whisper, 'Aren't you Sasha, Patty's daughter?' My instinct was to deny being my mother's daughter which was impossible when she added she was Seth's second cousin. She remembered seeing me at family gatherings, and more recently at Lorraine's funeral. When she asked how Ritchie was doing, I lied with brilliant ease that he was well. That satisfied her, and let me off the hook, or so I thought.

Two nights later, Ritchie turned up at my table, hurt written in his eyes. I agreed to meet him at the casino bar after my shift.

Beautiful cool jazz grooves wafted out of the bar. I was exhausted after being on my feet, in stilettos, for twelve hours. Richie sat at the corner window lost in thought. He did not hear me approach him and was startled when I touched his shoulder.

'Oh Sasha, sorry, I was a million miles away. Why did you leave without telling me?'

I ignored the expectation that I owed him an explanation of my choices.

'I'm having a vodka and lemonade, may I get you the same?'

Ritchie never drank a drop of alcohol in his life. Tonight he agreed to a drink, as I knew he would. Weak and compliant Ritchie!

I was determined to obliterate the memory of this night, and it seems I did. Before the week was over, I was back home riddled with guilt for running away. My mother ensured I fulfilled their promise to marry Ritchie, just as she decided to home-school the rebel in me. Here I was living in Ritchie's family home with his father. How this situation arose is beyond my understanding. My parents were across the street as they always were.

***

I GREW up in Lily Valley, a small elitist town, a hundred and fifty miles west of Plenitude City. I was an only child who lived in the shadows of my parent's lives. From the day the umbilical connection was severed, I had no breath to call my own. As a child, I was oblivious to the level of control my parents exerted. What I came to abhor was the persistent competition they set up with Lily Valley's youth. Nobody could be better than me because my parents had to feed their egos. Piano lessons, ballet, swimming, tennis, singing and signing up for every competition was how my childhood played out. Ritchie's parents were the sum of my family's intimate social circle.

Nobody else was good enough.

They disapproved of everything others did. It was either the houses people lived in, the schools their children attended, or the jobs they had that made my parents bitter and private.

Every summer we spent a week at a camp in the Raintree location. A group of approximately thirty families gathered each year to reconnect with their inner spirit. To the outsider, it was a wholesome retreat from the pressures of life. Uncle Seth ran the week of reconnecting with the self. Children under the age of sixteen were taken to the Dome, a large warehouse on the Raintree property. We played games, both physical and intellectual from badminton, gymnastics, swimming, chess, Head Full of Numbers, and Mancala.

At 6 pm we gathered with our families for dinner.

One summer when I was in my fifteenth year, I nursed a

sprained ankle after being too vigorous with the physical activities prescribed at the Dome. This prized me with the luxury of being allowed to stay alone in the loft where I slept. I was curious about the activities the adults engaged in and dragged myself to the loft window. From this position, I had an aerial view of the gathering and could hear every word uttered.

What I heard triggered my desire to get as far away as I could from this strange doctrine on lifestyle. At fifteen, I knew this was not how I wanted to live.

Uncle Seth, dressed in a white suit, held the microphone, and my mother sat in a chair behind him. My father was in the audience. Uncle Seth's eyes were closed, he looked serene, but what he advised churned my stomach.

'Beloveds, you have come this far and must carry the torch forward. It is incumbent upon you to ensure the next generation, your children, are nourished in our philosophy to carry the movement forward.'

The crowd of parents swayed and called out, 'Aye, so it shall be!'

My father stood up, and the room fell silent. I had a view of the back of his head.

'Master Seth, my wife, Patty, and I are ready to forge the pact on the union of our children Sasha and Ritchie. We agree they will be married as soon as each turns twenty. Sasha at twenty and Ritchie at twenty-one. We give you our word in acceptance of this proposition you made at their births. It is time to quell the burgeoning of their wild spirits. More noted in my daughter than your son.'

I froze. The crowd cheered and clapped like they were at a football match and the best goal was kicked. I had never heard Uncle Seth referred to as 'Master Seth,' by anyone before. I was exposed as something evil by my father! This was my first pry into what the purpose of this yearly sojourn entailed. Our parents convinced us that because we were their only children, they had sacrificed everything for us to feel what it was like to have a large family. More fathers stood up and echoed that they would take my father's lead in doing the same with their children. Each echoed a dire need to harness their daughters to be tamed by the men they chose.

Uncle Seth raised his hand for my father to approach him. He touched my father's head with a long gold rod and said he would be rewarded for leaving a legacy for a better future. A chant of the mission's thirteen affirmations followed. All members swayed as they said in unison:

> *We shall not step outside the teachings of the*
> *mission*
> *We shall not tarnish our values by sharing with*
> *others*
> *We shall only share our wealth and compassion*
> *within our community*
> *We shall not tolerate any transgressions from*
> *our children*
> *We shall work together tirelessly till death do*
> *us part*
> *We shall live in communities with our peers*
> *We shall encourage our children to take up*
> *skilled professions*
> *We shall remain exclusive against all odds*
> *We shall live by our constructed truth, accepting*
> *nothing else*
> *We shall surrender to none and marry within*
> *We shall uphold justice as we see fit*
> *We shall be written down in history*

We shall in time be the only way of the world

From this day on, the affirmations were repeated in our home. Every evening before we retired for the night this was imprinted in our minds. Sixteen was the year of my awakening to the things that did not sit well with me. I could not be selfish nor accept that I was exclusive, a cut above the rest of society. I suspected Ritchie agreed, but he did not dare to say so, not even to me.

We had no blood family. I wondered whether my parents had siblings and if my grandparents were alive. Whenever I asked these questions, my mother shut me down with lessons on gratitude for the life that she bestowed on me.

'Sasha, why do you ask these worthless questions? Are you not blessed for all that you have? What about Ritchie and his loving family? They are all the people we need.'

My parents never spoke of biological family. I pondered over this for years.

***

WHEN YOU ARE MADE to feel guilty for who you are throughout your childhood days when you fear you will lose your parents, you buckle, you do as you are told. And so, I married sweet, silent Ritchie. It was a frigid marriage. I felt care and compassion for him, not love that makes the pulse soar. I never knew that. I stayed in this cold relationship for five years until my father died.

Then the crushing blow.

Within two months of my father's passing, my mother married Uncle Seth at Raintree and moved across the street to live with Uncle Seth, Ritchie, and I.

This was the most unbearable time in my life.

I asked Ritchie for a divorce, but he, as always was mute on the matter. I told Uncle Seth and my mother that I was leaving. Both flew into a rage telling me I had to join the summer retreat to cleanse my mind of those wayward thoughts. I refused.

Uncle Seth ensured that I did not work outside the family home. I served father and son like a docile maid. I was twenty-five and sick of life. I struggled with breaking free but sunk into the pit of guilt as mounting responsibilities were thrown my way.

I remember the night I packed my bags to leave. It lives in my soul.

Ritchie, Uncle Seth, and my mother bound my legs and wrists and locked me in the upstairs bedroom. Ritchie and I never shared a bedroom in the five years of our clinical marriage. The choice our parents made to have us in separate rooms, saved my sanity. Why they did this is a mystery that has my profound gratitude.

Nobody looked for me.

Nobody questioned Ritchie, my mother, or Uncle Seth about my absence.

I was nobody to everybody.

I received three meals a day, left by Ritchie on my bedroom floor. He never looked at me. His eyes were fixed on the floor as they always had been.

One day the ensuite toilet in my room needed attention. A plumber arrived after my mother did a hurried cleanup of my room. I was told to wear my pyjamas and stay in bed coughing to let the plumber think I was unwell.

I peered at the man through a gap in the covers. He could have been in his mid-forties, soft-spoken and athletic looking. Uncle Seth told him that the doctor had ordered my bed rest and that I could not be moved. The man nodded averting his eyes from me.

The man asked for the water supply to be shut off.

Uncle Seth glanced in my direction and hurried out.

I hissed and the man stopped, not turning to where the sound came from.

'Please,' I whispered, 'help me, I am a prisoner here.'

Not a flinch, not a word from the man.

'Please I beg you, help me.'

I erupted in a coughing fit when Uncle Seth returned to the room.

'She's a hopeless case, does nothing to help herself.'

The man remained silent.

I lost hope of ever being rescued from this situation.

***

A WEEK LATER, well after 2 am I heard a faint tapping on my bedroom window. I thought birds were roosting on the window ledge. I heard the tapping again. After the initial tapping, it was two taps, then one, then two. I crept out of bed, careful not to knock anything over as I made my way to the window. I peeped through the slit in the curtain. It was him—the maintenance man! I was sure it was. He held up a note in his right hand with a torch in the other hand, balancing himself on the ladder he had moved from the side of the house. I squinted to read it.

Is what you said, true?

I nodded. I mouthed, *please help me.*

He mouthed back, *police?*

I nodded.

The dog next door took off in an unexpected barking frenzy, jumping up against the adjoining fence. The garden lights flicked on, exposing every nook and cranny. I heard hurried footsteps inside the house and rushed back to my bed.

My mother flung open my bedroom door. She bent over my bed and touched my forehead which she had never done before.

'She is asleep, Seth. The pills worked well on her.'

I tried to hold an even breathing rhythm. The last thing I needed was for Uncle Seth and my mother to sense my panic. I hoped the man on the ladder had got away.

I was awash with relief when I heard Uncle Seth say it was a false alarm, that a fox had agitated the neighbour's dog.

All I had to do was hope that the man would alert the police to get me out of this hellhole.

Nobody turned up to rescue me that night. Why would they? I was a nobody anyway. Born and raised with no freedom.

The next day, during the afternoon, I heard footsteps on the front porch. The doorbell rang and a male voice called out, 'It's the police here. Please let us in, we need to speak to you.'

My mother and Uncle Seth were out at a mission meeting that afternoon. My bad luck. I hung onto the hope that they would return. My snuffled sounds were inaudible.

I was gagged in a sealed room. Nobody would hear me, not even the neighbour's hypersensitive dog!

My mother shoved my dinner at my door around 7 pm that evening when I heard the doorbell ring, followed by a thumping on the gate. This time it was more than one voice. I heard a female voice call out, 'It's the local police, we're questioning the neighbourhood after some suspicious activities in the area last night.'

There was enough suspicious activity inside the house for sure! Were the police serious or was it a ploy to get the door opened to them?

I heard Uncle Seth say to my mother, 'Shut Sasha's bedroom door and turn on the music, I'll open the door.'

Over serene piano sounds, I heard voices but could not distinguish what the conversation was about. Then I heard footsteps in the hallway.

My gag was removed for dinner which meant I could yell, and yell I did!

'Help! Help! Get me out of here!'

The male police officer questioned, 'Who is that? Why is this door locked?'

What I heard Uncle Seth say is something I will never forget for the rest of my days, should I ever have the privilege of the rest of my days after this!

'That is our daughter. She is under psychiatric evaluation and her therapist has advised she remain in isolation as she is a danger to herself. You can speak to the psychiatrist if you wish. I can get him on the phone for you.'

'That won't be necessary, please open the door for us to assess her condition.'

'I'm sorry, we cannot do that. She might attack you and we do not want an accident if you think it necessary to turn your weapon on her to protect yourselves. She is our only daughter, and we are heartsore to isolate her this way. Please understand.'

Uncle Seth and my mother wept, begging that the police speak to my so-called psychiatrist.

'Give me her therapist's number and I will make that call down at the station. It's illegal to hold an adult person in the home against their will.'

I let out the loudest scream I could muster, fearful of what Uncle Seth would do to me once they left.

'Please don't leave me here. They will torture me. Seth is not my father!'

I was shattered when I heard the female officer up close to my door saying, 'I see what you mean, she is quite out of control. We will try for alternate arrangements for her treatment.'

I yelled again, 'Please, I beg you. I fear for my sanity, now my life. Don't leave without me!'

Silence.

No response to my plea. What is new in my life? Help was so close.

The house was quiet. Where were Uncle Seth and my mother?

I heard scraping sounds in the attic and my mother yelling, 'Hurry Seth, we must get her out of here right now before they return. We cannot take too much with us. Grab the essentials for a night or two until this dies down!'

My mother grabbed my legs pulling me out of bed, yelling at me to hurry, there was no time to dress. Once again, I was subjected to a command I hated!

Uncle Seth packed the car in the garage and shoved me in the back seat telling me to stay low.

What they did not expect was that the police officers

had called for backup and had barricaded the bottom of the driveway!

Ritchie was nowhere on the scene. He might have been tipped off to stay away until the hype died down. Uncle Seth and my mother assumed that this was a random check in the neighbourhood regarding suspicious activity.

In a frenzied rush of flashing lights, I was bundled into a police car and whisked away. I caught a glimpse of the horror on Uncle Seth's and my mother's faces.

Was this my freedom, here at last after a lifetime of incarceration?

The gruelling interview with Detective Sondra Tate and Inspector Emmanuel lasted six hours. Every detail that I could recall as a child up to the present moment was churned out of me.

I was never told whether Uncle Seth and my mother would face any charges.

Sondra Tate set me up in a motel with a mobile phone, blocked to all outgoing and incoming calls except her number. She told me to stay put until they could relocate me.

'Relocate? Where? You think my stepfather and mother will be on the hunt for me?'

'From what you've told Inspector Emmanuel and I, that husband of yours could be the one who hunts you down.'

'Ritchie? No, he only acts on what his father dictates.'

'Well, that's the point, right?'

'Won't Seth and my mother face charges, and perhaps jail time?'

'Charges, yes, prison, unlikely. You faced emotional abuse and were physically locked in the house, so technically, because they provided your accommodation and meals, the justice system in this county will give them a light penalty.'

'Ah, that's why I'm being relocated.'

Sondra Tate studied my face and said nothing.

***

THE MOTEL ROOM was run down—the curtains sagged with decades of dust, bleached by the sun. I held my nose as I peered through the window. A white SUV skulked across the street. I pulled back breaking into a series of sneezes. Was I being watched? A text message to Detective Sondra Tate settled my fear.

> An unmarked car with an officer on the
> watch for your safety.

If I entertained any thoughts of relocating myself, they were dashed.

I had no control of my life for the entirety of my life, and now I was nowhere near making decisions for myself. I lay awake dreaming of the life I wanted.

In all the visions that crossed my mind's eye that restless night...I was alone.

***

THREE YEARS LATER...

This time I crossed the physical border into the eastern

state with a new name, new look, and a handsome man in my life. I was now Robin Matthews.

Detective Sondra Tate did everything possible to make Sasha disappear. My dark, straight hair was blonde and tightly curled. I was given a history that I had to memorise and own. I was an orphan with a big dream of being a writer. After an inheritance from an aunt, I did not know I had, I moved to the eastern state to live in the villa she had left me. I took a writing course at the local college for a year to launch my writing career. Sondra Tate kept in touch throughout this time, warning me never to write about my experience. She kept me in the dark about what my mother and Seth's fate were. As for Ritchie, who knows what became of him? I am free as Robin Matthews... Seth is still Seth, and my mother is always, Patty. I worked hard to wash away the torment of those years to be my own person.

In this new life, I have all I could ever want, but I'm still not me. I'm a fabricated person known as Robin Matthews. I have a birth certificate to that effect. The title deed to the villa property is in my fabricated name.

Two years into this new life I met a wonderful man who asked me to marry him. I refused. He stuck around and we have been together since then. He asks no questions and I tell him no lies. I have been schooled to conceal the truth. Sondra Tate's briefings on who Robin Matthews should be, framed my fictitious identity.

Things ran smoothly, I had a police force-appointed hairdresser who called at the house every month to keep my locks blonde. Judd, my partner, knew I dyed my hair and never questioned it. We live in separate homes, yet in most things, we are like a married couple. Judd is a college professor. I met him when I took the creative writing course when I first arrived in town. We met quite by chance one evening at his book launch a year after I had finished the course. It started as a friendship, but his kindness and compassion stole my heart. His father died when he was five years old. The bond he shared with his mother was one I desired. She is in a nursing home. Judd visits her every day after work, and I have visited her with him on Sundays. Her question was always, 'When are you and Judd going to make me a grandmother?' Judd answered, 'Soon, mother, soon.' As Robin, I knew that even though Sasha had disappeared, there was no way I could bring a child into the world if I had no closure on my past.

I was living a lie.

Judd and I loved the outdoors. We hiked in the nearby forest and spent most weekends at the beach. When he asked me to travel with him to Canada for a conference, I had to lie about my flying phobia. My relocation clause was never to leave town unless approved by Detective Sondra Tate, and her supervisor.

Judd was persistent.

'We could get a sedative prescribed for you so that you sleep for the duration of the flight. Would you give that some thought?'

'I don't think I can... it's been a childhood fear for some reason. Please don't ask me to consider counselling either. I just cannot do it.'

Judd backed off. I could tell it saddened him that I was resolute on the matter.

Nothing was solid in my life.

Any day, Sondra Tate could ask me to be ready to move to a new location. I knew I would never be Sasha again in this life.

King Lear was playing in the neighbouring town and Judd booked an evening session with a dinner package.

I tucked into my seafood paella and glass of red. It was a warm evening, and the restaurant was crowded. The air was heavy with spices, and I felt faint. Judd touched my arm.

'Are you ok, Robin? You look flushed. Do you want to go outside for some air?'

I felt wretched but had no intention of ruining Judd's evening

'I'm good, it's just a tad warm in here. Soon we will be in an airy theatre.'

Judd whispered, leaning over the table, 'A woman at the left corner table is staring you out, I wonder whether she might know you.'

I tried not to be obvious and turned slowly to observe the starer.

Her eyes were saucers when I turned around. She looked familiar. Her face gave nothing away by way of recognition of who I was.

'I don't know her. '

'Why don't you take a walk up to her and ask if you two have met before.'

'No way, I can't do that, it's invasive.'

'Invasive, how?'

'She might be looking our way with curiosity, or she could be in a reverie, you know, not really seeing.'

'True. Sorry, I don't mean to ruin your evening, so forget it.'

I studied Judd's face. He did not appear ruffled by my reaction, but I had my guard up. The woman was looking my way because she recognised me. I had no idea who she was. I had to call Sondra Tate. Those were her instructions the minute I perceived anything or anyone from my past nearby.

I excused myself from the table, telling Judd I had to go to the ladies' room. Sweet, caring Judd could be stifling when he thought I was unwell.

'I'll walk over with you and wait outside the ladies' room. You are a little unwell tonight.'

Another hot flush surged to my cheeks. This is the last thing I needed now!

'No that won't be necessary, I'll be back in a flash.'

Judd said no more and went back to his paella.

I locked myself in a cubicle and sent a text message to Sondra Tate. The exterior door to the powder room swung open. I waited for the person to shut themselves in a cubicle before I stepped out.

Nothing... silence...deadly silence...

I had to get out before Judd came over to check up on me.

I rushed out with no intention of stopping at the wash basin when I saw the staring woman waiting at the entrance. She grabbed my arm.

'Excuse me, sorry I don't mean to be rude, but you remind me of someone I knew. She disappeared a few years ago.'

'I'm sorry, I suppose we all have a twin somewhere in the world. Pardon me, I must get back to my table.'

I unhooked my arm from her grip but she had one more thing to say.

'There's something in your eyes, height, not your voice, that reminds me of my cousin Ritchie's wife, Sasha.'

A ton of bricks hit me in the chest, 'I'm sorry, it must be hard for you, to lose someone, but I must go, my husband's waiting for me. Enjoy your evening.'

I threw the last line in to draw her off my scent. Who was she?

Judd knew I was anxious when I fell into the chair and told him we had to leave the restaurant.

'What's wrong, Robin?'

'The woman you pointed out, followed me to the ladies' room and grabbed my arm as I was leaving.'

'What? Whatever for? Did she speak to you?'

'Let's get out of here, I'll tell you what happened when we are in the theatre.'

We grabbed our jackets and made a beeline for the door.

It was an hour before the show. We sat in the theatre foyer.

Judd listened to my edited version of what happened with the woman and agreed it was weird behaviour from the stranger.

'Forget it, let's just enjoy the show.'

My phone buzzed. Now was an awkward time to check my messages.

When Judd went to get a drink, I did a quick check through my messages. Sondra Tate's words placed me in a predicament.

Get out of the area now!

Judd returned and I feigned feeling faint.

'You stay on and watch the play. I'll catch a cab home.'

'I can't let you go off alone when you're faint. I'll come with you. We can always catch the play some other time. '

'I feel awful if you miss out.'

'No arguments missy, let's go!'

Judd was everything I needed in my life—caring and

selfless. If only it was him and never Ritchie, Seth, and yes, I can say it without remorse, my mother. She created this situation I live with day after day. My greatest fear is Judd finding out about my past, that my name is a fabrication, and leaving me. He is the most authentic person I know.

I am a fake.

I waited for Sondra Tate's call for advice on my next move.

***

SONDRA TATE CALLED at 8 pm.

'Robin, what were you doing out and about in the next town during carnival week when hordes of city folk attend these events?'

'Judd booked us dinner and the theatre. We got there in the evening to avoid daylight carnival events. So, what happens now?'

'You must stay at home for two weeks without leaving the house. The story is you are in quarantine with a bad case of chickenpox.'

'Chickenpox!'

'That's the only way to stop anyone visiting you, that is if you do get visitors.'

'You know I lead a reclusive life. What do I tell Judd?'

'The same story, Robin, unless you want to come clean with him. Do you trust him with knowledge of your past?'

'That's a tough one. I do trust him with all my heart. I'm not ready to let him know I'm a fake.'

'Not a fake, Robin, but someone who is staying safe from the dangers of a past life.'

'Are there still dangers, as you say? I am tired of this cat-and-mouse game.'

'It's no game. Think about what you want to tell Judd, but if you are holding your truth from him, then chickenpox it is, I'm afraid.'

JUDD WAS PREPARING a paper for an upcoming conference. I decided I would tell him I was feeling unwell. Then, work out what truth I will construct. Either way, I'm living a deceptive life, if he knows the truth and can't handle it, I have no control over that.

This concealed life has toughened me for anything.

AT 10 PM Judd looked in on me before he left.

'Hey, you are in bed early tonight!'

'I don't feel well, I'm warm and have a pounding headache.'

I said I told Judd no lies, and here I was lying like a con artist to the man who loved me as much as I loved him.

'Are you still stressing over that strange encounter at the restaurant?'

'No! Not at all.'

I protested too much, and half expected Judd to pick up on that.

'I'm glad to hear that. May I get you something to drink before I head off? If you allowed me to stay over, I could take care of you tonight.'

'Thank you, kind sir. I think I'll sleep instead and might feel brand new in the morning.'

'Ah, the miracle of sleep. I'll leave you now, but promise you will call me if you feel you're getting worse.'

'I will, thank you. You are too kind for your good, you know.'

'Cut the crazy talk, I love you, and that's what people do when they love each other. I know you would do the same for me.'

I smiled and nodded and soon heard his car reversing out of my driveway. I tossed and turned. My head churned with memories of Ritchie, Seth, and my mother. I stared at the ceiling, feeling hopeless and annoyed that my life was still abnormal.

At 7:30 AM, Judd called.

'How was your night?'

Poor Judd, he knew I abhorred terms of endearment and dropped 'honey,' 'darling' and whatever else lovers called each other. I found it fake and did not want to add that to my already fake life.

'I must call Dr Larsen,' I croaked, 'I was burning up all night.'

'I told you to call me, Robin. I could cancel my morning meeting and drive you over to Dr Larsen.'

'No, don't do that. I'll call him and take it from there. Please don't cancel your meeting.'

'Call me, once you know what's going on with the fever.'

I don't deserve this human being, so kind and loving while I'm lying and about to escalate the lie.

. . .

LATER THAT MORNING when Judd heard that I had chickenpox, he was devastated that we would be apart for two weeks. He had never had chickenpox as a child and could easily catch it from me. I told him another convincing lie.

I lived and breathed the lie of my fabricated life. How was I ever going to untangle myself from this mess? I was deception personified in my intimate relationship. I had played out many times, telling Judd about my past life. In all the visions and versions of that truth-telling, he walked out on me. Even when thinking about truth, I'm inclined to offer versions of it. My gut feeling that Judd would walk out on me, kept me determined to hold onto the truth, a while longer. The stranger in the restaurant was a live threat to my relationship with him if she chose to find me. I tried to imagine her face and drew a blank on who she might be. I should have given her a chance to tell me who she was. Fear makes one act in unexpected ways. The woman might be from Seth's church, but I could not put a name to her face. Had I blocked that part of my life to the extent that although she knew me, I had no idea who she was?

Memory, after trauma is a force to be reckoned with, I guess. I found myself forgetting the details of that torrid time in my life.

I spent two weeks wrestling with thoughts on how I could remove the thorns from my life. I was never at rest.

I called Sondra Tate in the middle of the second week of my fake isolation.

'I cannot do this anymore. I cannot live this life. I want out of this protection program.'

'Your safety will be at risk if you do, I can't hold you to the program if you are unwilling, but Seth and your mother were not convicted because of a loophole that worked in their favour.'

'I'm the victim, yet I'm a prisoner in my skin, and they walk free. Thank you for all you've done, Detective Tate, but I'd rather be dead than live like this anymore. It's not a life.'

'I know how you feel, Robin, but you entered the program willingly, just remember that. What you choose to do now will be blood on my hands.'

'Not for a second will I blame you for anything. I did enter willingly and now I'm choosing to walk away. Judd deserves the truth, and I will take whatever comes my way. I don't want to be Robin. I will go back to being Sasha and face what may come.'

'Why don't you wait it out to the end of this quarantine period and reassess? Think it through, before you act.'

'No, I've had enough time to think and overthink my life. I want to be free.'

'There will be paperwork to fill out so it's not as if you are free from the protection program, because you say you want to be, please understand that. I recommend you talk to Judd first and then decide.'

'I intend to speak to Judd, right away, and regardless of the outcome with him, I will file the paperwork to opt out.'

'I hear you loud and clear, Robin. Keep me posted.'

She hung up before I could say, 'Sasha, please, not Robin.'

I decided to give myself a day before I invited Judd over.

***

THE HARDEST THING I had to do in this life, was to tell Judd he was in love with a fraud. To tell him I was Sasha, not Robin. After many cups of coffee that night, I decided the best way to reveal the truth was to begin at the beginning and explain why I am at this point in my life.

I called Judd and lied again that my doctor said I was over the infectious period and that it was fine for him to come over.

'Are you sure, I'm not worried about myself? I don't want to bring anything to you that I might have been exposed to if you are in a vulnerable state.'

'Just please, please come over, we must talk face-to-face, it's important to what decision you might have to take.'

'Robin! What is going on, it sounds like you intend to break it off with me. Why?'

This was the first time in our two years together that I heard anxiety in Judd's voice.

'Come over. All will be explained. Firstly, I don't have chickenpox. There! I've said it!'

His silence on the other end of the line was a slow death. I heard him sigh, and whisper, 'I'll be there in thirty minutes. Can I bring you anything? Have you had dinner?'

'Just yourself, Judd, thanks. I have dinner prepared if you care to still break bread with me after our talk.'

He drew a deep breath, 'Just stop the mind games, I'll see you soon.'

Another first, the phone was plonked down on me. Was this a sign of what would happen after our talk? Anxiety? Silence? No communication?

True to form, thirty minutes later, Judd rang my doorbell.

I greeted his red hang-dog-face, 'You should have let

yourself in like you always do. Why did you ring the doorbell?'

'I don't know. I feel I'm being relegated to an outsider.'

'Don't be silly, now. Come in.'

I pulled his left arm. He resisted, then allowed me to lead him in. His face was etched with uncertainty, his eyes holding fear. Firsts, I had never seen in Judd before.

I ran through everything beginning with the woman who said she thought I was familiar at dinner just two weeks ago, all the way to Seth, Ritchie, and my mother. A large portion of my revelation was on the cult my parents belonged to.

I held Judd's hands and stared into his eyes. 'I will accept that you will want to walk out now, and never return. It will hurt until the end of my days not to have you in my life. But I will understand whatever you choose to do from this point on.'

He was wide-eyed and trembling.

'You're scaring me. Say something, please.'

'Er...I would be lying if I did not say my world, our world together, crumbled in this moment... my head is a mess...'

'I get it, Judd, I will always love you and feel it's only right I set you free.'

'Set me free? Why are you saying this?'

'Because I understand that the very thing you believed no longer exists.'

'I did not say that. I said my head is a mess, and our world, the world I thought I knew with you, was not really as it seemed. Please allow me to digest this. I don't want to leave, I love you, and none of this was ever your fault.'

My eyes burned, and an uncontrollable sob from the depths of my being gushed forth. I dropped to the floor and let the tsunami gush. Judd knelt beside me, cradling me. We lay there until sunrise. It was the first night he had ever stayed over at my place. We spent the next day with me recalling and reliving in minute detail what my life was like before I met him.

'You are the bravest person I know, and I appreciate that you wanted to break the binding protocol to tell me your hidden secret, but I'm far gladder that you upheld your safety. We should move out of town and restart your life by whatever name you choose to call yourself. That is if you want that life with me.'

I nodded, but not a word passed my lips. My emotions were close to erupting each time Judd's compassion and acceptance washed over me.

DETECTIVE SONDRA TATE came over to discuss relocating me. I refused to ask Judd to leave while she briefed me. He was part of my healing, he knew my truth, and by abundant grace, he wanted to stay in my life.

Sondra Tate was not happy with our plan to relocate on our terms.

'It's still risky, especially because someone noticed you, not so long ago, and knew you.'

'We plan to leave the country, marry and pick up a life that my love can live with ease. No fear. No secrets.'

'Marry...'

Judd looked at me with a nod and wink, 'Yes, I took the liberty of assuming you will accept me. Trust me I did not intend to propose, again, this way.'

'There's one problem though, aren't you still married to Ritchie.' Sondra Tate said.

'That can be annulled with immediate effect!' Judd piped in.

'It should have been done a long time ago, but I was too afraid to ask again. I will find a lawyer who works together with the protection program to ensure that I'm not shooting myself in the foot.'

I felt good planning my life.

'I don't think that's necessary, work it out through Detective Tate. Am I right Detective? You created the program for Robin, and you have all the information on Robin's case. At some point, I'm going to have to call you, Sasha.'

'I intend reverting to my Sasha identity. Robin is dead.' I looked directly at Detective Sondra Tate, 'I want out of this program and wonder whether I will retain access to your services.'

Judd butted in again, this time as though Detective Sondra Tate had left the room. My knees were weak and my heart raced. Why was he assuming the lead here? I did not want, nor needed his interference now. He could ruin any hope I had for my freedom.

'You are part of a national security arm of the protection program, and it goes without saying, or doubting that you have a right to be protected. I'm surprised this annulment was not suggested a long time ago, after all, that you have endured.'

Judd was frank when I needed to hear reason. My judgement and knowledge of the wider world had dulled with darting between the shadows and light. My lie sheltered me from the reality of the world. It was time to be free. I had to steer the course my life should take. I wanted to do it on *my* terms. I did not need another Seth assuming control of my life. Richie had no voice and left me in the snake pit. I loved Judd but had to find a way to tell him to leave things to me.

'Let's leave this here for today. I'll be in touch on how best to expedite what *you* want, Robin.' Sondra Tate threw Judd a long, hard stare as she left.

I agreed and knew I had to tell Judd to back off. Somehow. He did not deserve ingratitude from me for all he had done for me.

Judd was surprised when I asked him to stay at his place until things were clearer on all matters. I needed to straighten up my life. Perfection does not exist, but I had to clear unfinished business.

The sudden shift in Judd's ever-so-amenable manner, I must admit, floored me. Why was he jumping into command into that part of my life that he only became aware of, now, in this minute?

It disturbed me. A restless night left me worse for wear.

Thoughts of being trapped again, and Judd's assumption that now I would accept his marriage proposal, left me frazzled. I loved him. I needed a clear head to move forward to freedom.

Marriage scared me. My parents were far from ideal partners. Did that even exist, for anyone? Perfection, what a load of nonsense! When a cult is the only binding factor between a husband and wife, it made me dubious about their love for each other. With that in mind, I questioned my non-existent authority on a good marriage.

On that final thought, my gut, my heart and my mind told me I had to refuse Judd's proposal. I was happy to remain as we were. I had my space—well if one could call it space with my hidden identity, seclusion, and the constant threat that I could be called to move to a new location at any time.

Detective Sondra Tate asked for a few days to check on my marital status with Ritchie, then legal proceedings would begin.

Judd came over at the crack of dawn, breakfast in hand as usual. I was anxious and fidgety. He was calm and cheerful.

'Soon we will be Mr and Mrs How wonderful!'

'Judd, look. ... I don't want to make any plans until I know if I can extricate myself from my past.'

'What do you mean, Robin? Are you flirting with going back to that life?'

I looked at him agog. Where did that ridiculous notion come from? Heat sparked through me, rising to my eyeballs. My palms were clammy.

'I ...I cannot believe you just said that...'

His eyes grew larger than I had ever seen. His unsmiling face and glazed eyes sent a shiver rippling through me to cool the heat that had just risen.

'Well, why else will you delay our future together.'

'I want to be sure that nothing is binding in that past heinous marriage that will damage your reputation or hurt you in any way. You don't know Seth and the clan as I do.'

'You have the police on your side, what harm could I come to? I don't get why you are still afraid of them.'

'Seth and my mother got off on some technicality. The clan has a devious, smart legal arm. I'm just saying we must be careful.'

'I thought you wanted your freedom to live again. But it seems you have accepted living in the shadows.'

How could he say these things to me? Where was the Judd I knew? His mercurial flip in the last twenty-four hours messed up my head and emotions.

We barely touched the breakfast in front of us.

'I'll let you be to think things over. Call me once you decide what you want.' He stood up, and looked down at me—there was something so cold and final in his words.

At this crossroad, I realised that freedom must be on my terms. Judd provided the validation I needed. He made me feel whole. Whole in the lie that made me Robin. I felt safe as Robin but lacked self-definition. I was Robin, created by Detective Sondra Tate.

If I allowed myself to overthink what was right for me, my heart would outsmart the reason I needed.

I did not need voices of control.

I wrote a note to Judd and one to Sondra Tate. Thank you notes. I did owe them my life, I suppose.

I left the house I had started to call home and crossed the border into my eastern state. This time it was not a dream. My flight to Venezuela was booked. It was on my bucket list from the day I was forced to marry Ritchie.

A new passport and a new life awaited me as Mercy Knight ready to cut my path!

Dear reader, someday, perhaps...I might return to let you know if I found happiness. Happiness that I want on my terms.

Until then, be free, be you. Always.

WATCHING

Running away is a necessary cowardly act. If the past is confronted, the present acknowledged, then peace arrives to still an overthinking mind. In simplicity there is authenticity and good mental health.

WATCHING

I watched without knowing I was being watched.

I MOVED to the small town of Hoppington after living and working as an attorney for fifteen years.

I couldn't do it anymore. My hair fell out and dark circles gave me a panda-eyed look that was far from becoming! Late nights, weekend work, and an ever-increasing inbox with no end in sight eroded my joy. Don't get me wrong, I loved doing what I did. My workaholic tendency made me a prime target for abuse from lazy colleagues at Vandruit-In-Law. They passed everything and anything my way.

I chose a single life for reasons my colleagues did not know but assumed was my choice to advance my career. When you work with domestic violence day after day, week after week, year in and year out, it saps all personal time. I valued seeing women get on their feet again, bolder, and better, after a tumultuous relationship. This is not why I chose to avoid romantic relationships. That is another issue.

The emotional investment in my career left no space for life. Added to this is that I am a people pleaser. That sucked the lifeblood from me. I could not switch off from the job, and people's demands. Some call it a blessing if one is vested in a self-sacrificing work of passion. A spiritual thing perhaps, I don't know to be honest. Constant trips inter-state claimed my weekends after endless weekdays in late-night meetings. It was a 5 am start every day. As the chosen one I was called upon to support and entertain visiting legal eagles—gruelling, to say the least.

I hated hearing folk around me constantly say, 'Moira's ok, she has no domestic responsibilities, no school run, no sports weekends, no needy partner. Wish I had her life.'

Fifteen years of the same voices had to get to me at some stage. I started my career as a bright-eyed young thing dreaming that I would be a courtroom dynamo standing up to everything from sexism, racism, abuse, and corporate corruption. I could go on. I desired to do it all, be the best, the first at everything.

Fifteen years later, here I am in Hoppington, a place with one main road in and out, one coffee shop, one butcher, and a fruit and vegetable market, a tiny grocery store, packed with everything from hardware to bread. The barber groomed human heads and furry friends!

I left my high-flying city life and its pretentious para-phernalia to work on my soul. How I was going to do that with the baggage I carried? It seemed like the right thing to do at this point in my life. Burnt-out, stressed point in my life.

I was alone in my Hoppington cottage with only my

thoughts for company. I relished the first weeks in the town, getting up when I wanted, eating or not eating as I chose. Unpacked boxes crowded my two-bedroom cottage with no inclination to do anything about it. Three weeks later I knew I had to venture out to get to know my surroundings. I took a two-year lease on the property online and moved within a fortnight of signing the paper-work. The real estate advertisement called it *a touch of paradise to renew body, mind, and spirit.* I was sold on that promise.

I was nervous at the thought of stepping into an unknown space. City life was in some ways an escape from being singled out. Here I would be noticed if anything, as the newcomer, the outsider, perhaps? The real estate agent said if I desired privacy and solitude then Hoppington was the place for me.

I dressed in black pants and a grey sweater. A sign of my colourless inner state. It was a cold morning. A black beanie pulled over my locks and finished the look. My light brown hair was thanks to my mother, but my dark skin was an unknown genetic throwback. That is what I came to accept. With no siblings to confirm if this was a dominant trait, I let it slip to the back of my overloaded mind.

My front garden was a tiny strip, not large enough to be called a garden, perhaps a nature strip, who knows. I have never been a garden enthusiast. The grass was green and well-groomed. A gardener was scheduled to come in once a month. I had to do the tidy-up in between. A red post box, propped up on the white wooden fence that wrapped its way around this small block, made my new abode pleasing to the eye. 43 Dorset Lane, a hidden beauty, tucked away at the furthest end of the lane. Forgotten. That is what I chose, to be, forgotten, by all and sundry who demanded so much of me.

It was a clear, blue-skied morning with a chill in the air that was cold enough to make me shiver under my warm attire. Not a soul was in sight at 10 am on a still Sunday morning. Just what I needed to peruse, unnoticed, through this little town. The birds across the meadow from my place, the only lives awake, twittered in a frenzy, noticing my newness. I glanced at the houses along Dorset Lane, all four of them. Curtains were drawn, and verandas were empty. In the distance, a dog barked. I quickened my step. The main road into town intersected with Dorset Lane. I walked along the shopping strip. Nothing was open. I craved a takeaway coffee, but no city privilege was to be had at this hour. 10 am! I would have had my second cup by now on the run to work. The butcher was closed with a *Back on Monday* sign on the door. The bakery was shut, but movement inside the tiny grocery store was hard to miss. I veered down a side road and each turn I took met with the same serene stillness. I headed back up the main road and found the grocery shop open.

I stepped inside.

The warm smell of bread baking was welcoming. A cheery voice called out from behind a trinket-laden countertop.

'Good morning, you are an early bird!'

A set of pixie eyes peered above the trinkets.

'Oh, there you are! Good morning. I'm a newbie in town so I guess I must get used to the later start around here.'

'Ah, you're the newcomer at 43 Dorset Lane. You've been here a few weeks, right?'

I shivered at the lack of privacy. Privacy I was promised by the Real Estate Agent. In my need to get away from overwhelming city pressure, I did not consider what my mother bemoaned as small-town gossip. She was born and raised in this rural community. Bright city lights pulled her away from rolling meadows and country lanes. She started her singing career in this town, met the wrong fella, had me, and died when I was sixteen years old.

Here I was going back to where she came from.

Nobody in town knew I was Harriet's daughter. I wanted to keep it that way. All her surviving relatives had wandered out of their rural origins to seek fame and fortune. That is what she told me. I don't know any of them by name or face.

She kept my birth a secret.

The interesting pixie eyes behind the counter belonged to a toothless old guy called Jetson.

'Hear you are a big shot lawyer from the city.'

'Word gets around fast in these parts! Lawyer, yes, big shot, I don't think so,' I laughed.

'Anyways dear, welcome to Hoppington if nobody has done that already. Not much hopping going on around here except for the spring dance that's coming up in a few weeks. Hope you'll join us.'

'I love a quiet place. I'll have to think about the spring dance, as I don't have anything snazzy to wear for such an event.'

'Oh, you ladies worry too much about that. My missus, she didn't care about any of that. She's dead ten years now.'

His matter-of-fact attitude to his wife's passing surprised me. I only ever experienced my mother's death which left me scarred to this day. It might be the reason I chose to come to her hometown, perhaps to heal.

'I'm sorry, you must miss your wife. Do you have children?'

'Ten years is a long time. I did my grieving. Time heals you know. No children. She did not want any and I respected that. The pain she endured from her siblings left her scarred. A terrible lot.'

Jetson was a talker, and I had my backup. Talkers in my experience could not keep a lid on it even if you asked them to hold it close. I knew nothing about this community. Harriet never spoke about her childhood here.

'What are your plans, will you stay on like us folk, or are you here briefly, escaping something?'

The twinkle in his eye confirmed he wanted me to be open about my life on why I chose to move here. He would get none of that from me. I had too much I wanted to keep locked from wagging tongues.

'I'm not sure yet. I wanted a change so here I am.'

His long hard look told me he suspected I was lying.

'I must be off now, you have a good day, Jetson, sir. I'll be around again.'

He beamed, a glow radiating through his wan cheeks.

'Have a good day, Miss Moira, or is it Mrs?'

'Just Moira,' I winked and had him chuckling like a shy teenager.

I had not introduced myself to him, yet he knew I was Moira, a *big-shot lawyer from the city*. What I did not know was that Jetson would play an important role in my time at Hoppington.

I strolled back down the main road. The coffee shop was open for business. I smiled at the curious faces casting a look my way. One close encounter almost into my personal life was enough. I hurried back to 43 Dorset Lane to brew my coffee.

I spent a quiet afternoon unpacking boxes although thoughts on whether I wanted to set roots here for a time made me uneasy. The situation at Vandruit-in-Law was hush-hush, but things had a way of slipping out. The media had no inkling at the outset about what transpired, so Vandruit, with no pun on 'In-Law,' was still open for business. I had to leave. Long hours were one thing, but reputation is an entirely different thing. That was something my dear mother upheld. I had no family, and no family law business was going to take me down.

All I knew was that Harriet referred to my unknown father as Gordon. She sang in pubs and clubs but never brought men home like people thought she would. Her values made her an oddity among the people she worked with. Raising me and giving me a good education and a loving home was all she wanted. If she had another man, I knew nothing about it. What her life was like in her younger years remained her mystery.

The spring dance Jetson mentioned had me worried. Would I be thought a snob if I chose not to attend? Should I remain behind closed doors until after the dance? There were two weeks to month end, anyway... Here I was doing it again, overthinking everything. This is what I wanted to leave behind in the city. I turned on some relaxing smooth Sunday jazz and unpacked a few more boxes.

A photo frame of Harriet and I, taken on my sixteenth birthday, peered up from a box marked 'nostalgia'. Two days after that photograph was taken, my mother died. My eyes welled up seeing her beautiful smile. She sacrificed her youth to raise me. I missed her. Twenty-nine years does not erase the pain. Jetson questioned if I came to Hoppington to escape. Who escapes from such a great loss when you are left entirely alone with no one to call family? Not even a remote relative. I had to shake this feeling. Depression sucked any hope of happiness in my last two years of high school. I chose to live alone. Harriet left me the house and a sizeable bank balance that I did not have to take on part-time work as I struggled through two years of school without her. I ducked and dived from social services detection during that time. University life helped me cope with my grieving heart. Studying law was her dream for me, and I enjoyed it.

All four seasons passed through Hoppington in a day. The late afternoon air was warm. I ventured onto the porch, gin and tonic in hand and Toni Morrison's collection of essays, *The Source of Self Regard*. I needed her advice to renew a sense of my self-regard. In the last six months at Vandruit-in-Law, I was a shadow of my easy-going but hardworking nature. I lay awake most nights willing sleep to come to no avail. I crawled out of bed, downed a mug of black coffee, after a hot shower, and trudged to work. The law firm was a thirty-minute walk from my apartment. I lived close to the office because of the frequent crack of dawn and late-night meetings most days of the week. I rented our family home to a mother and daughter which I thought fitting to honour Harriet. Perhaps I should have gone back there when I needed space and renewal. I did not believe burnout would claim me. Stress and emotional factors related to my self-worth burdened my long days. What a fool I was to think my work was good enough to gain the respect of the top brass in the firm. Fool indeed! My mother was careful with who she chose to trust and with whom she invested her time.

My mind wafted to the past often since my arrival in Hoppington. It must be her spirit drawing me in even though she turned her back on her hometown. During this mental meandering, I was aware of the hunched figure across at number 40. I squinted in the afternoon sun convincing myself that the figure was hunched over a book, reading. That made me wonder if there was a library or bookstore in town. The figure did not look up once in my direction.

The sky was a brilliant blue and the afternoon sun fell softly across the meadow, nuzzling grassy tips of carpet-like undulations. Everything was still, tranquil, almost perfect. At that moment I was resolved to get involved in this small community if I was allowed. Jetson was lovely enough in his way. I pondered whether it was only an older population that lived here. Did the younger folk stay on, or leave as my mother did?

As I turned to go inside the house, I stole a backward glance at number 40. The figure had moved away. My interest was piqued. What did country folk do? Bake a cake and take it over, introduce myself and then invite them over? A little voice in my head advised that I should get to know the people first. Perhaps a weekday stroll into the shopping area for a cup of coffee and breakfast was a starting point. Tomorrow was too soon. Perhaps Tuesday or Wednesday morning. Caution was my middle name. This is what I was told by my manager at the law firm. I was also good at walking away from associations that tested my set ways. That resulted in a very small band of friends that never got too close. I chose that. My city neighbour, Erica, called me once since my arrival in Hoppington. I kept the conversation superficial. She wanted to know if I had met the townsfolk yet. When she said, 'Moira, you need to open up to the people there. Quit being cautious.' I agreed but knew I would not be calling her for a while. It always baffled me how people dropped labels they were not invited to attach. A bit of familiarity opened the door to judgement. I should stop overthinking. It will lead me down the rabbit hole of depression. Let's wait and see what Tuesday or Wednesday morning brings. I'm optimistic.

A night of dreams took me back to the firm.

Vandruit senior was in his seventies, a cold-hearted, mean man to his son-in-law, Fabian. Now you get the 'In-Law' aspect of the firm. Fabian held the business together with his ethical approach to all justice matters. You would think that is the only way, right? Vandruit senior was something else. He crossed the boundaries of what was legal on many matters that had me believe he had the county judge on his payroll. Fabian and Vandruit were equal partners in the business after he married Vandruit's only daughter. Things turned sour for Fabian when his wife died. The death of his daughter unleashed the nasty side of Vandruit. He challenged staff members who refused to work on apparent illegal matters. The values he upheld when he interviewed me for the position handling domestic cases, evaporated when he cremated his daughter. He was tied to Fabian and made it known he wanted him out of the partnership. That was my lesson on the many faces people display when things change in their lives. Vandruit's words rang out in my dream, *Moira, I'm counting on you to support me on ALL decisions I make in this firm. Is that clear?* I felt like a child who would be punished if I had a different opinion. My nodding in response to his command was a fatal error. He held me to it. Little did I know how far he would go to get his way? That began my dark days at the firm. The man who interviewed me all those years ago was warm, upstanding, and fatherly in a way. Did I nod because I thought I owed him for employing me? I carried allegiance like a neon light affixed to my head. The choices we make, the things we agree to, led by some misguided allegiance, creep up on you in ways you never think possible.

In the winter of July 2000, Fabian left the office around 9 pm. I was the last one to lock up and leave. That night was his last at the firm.

He never returned.

I was the only one who saw him that night. He left fifteen minutes before I did.

My life was never the same when Fabian vanished.

I was not close to anyone in the firm. I had no confidant.

Tonight the horror returned. It had slipped out of consciousness in my flurry of packing and moving to Hoppington. I turned on the bedside reading lamp and reached for Toni Morrison's essays.

***

MONDAY SLIPPED by with more unpacking. I decided that Tuesday would be my breakfast morning on the main road. It would allow me to get a feel for the locals. I slipped into a pair of jeans, joggers, and a baggy white tee shirt. When I stepped onto the porch, my eyes drifted across to number 40, and there was the hunched figure again. This time with a large-brimmed hat. I tied up my laces and headed off past number 40. My eyes remained on the figure. I had every intention of raising my hand in greeting. The bent head remained down. I stole past, relieved I did not have to smile or get drawn into small talk.

The main shopping road was busier than it was on Sunday. The bakery, coffee shop, and Jetson's supermarket were open. The coffee shop appeared empty. A lady of middle years was at the counter. She greeted me with a broad smile.

'Good morning, welcome. What can I get you? We have the finest coffee and fresh scones if that's what you're after.'

'Hello! I'd love some of that fine coffee and breakfast please.'

'That's what I like to hear. Breakfast is always the best start to any day. The menu is on the table of your choice. We have the best bacon, locally sourced, as are our eggs. You couldn't ask for anything fresher here in Hoppington.'

Her exuberance was beginning to unnerve me. I selected a table at the furthest end of the cafe. The menu was basic, and I was happy with scrambled eggs and bacon. The local community paper stared at me, asking to be read.

The headline screamed *Spring Dance*. Tickets were available at all retail stores. All four of them, were the bakery, coffee shop, grocery store and butcher.

The woman returned with my breakfast.

'I'm Juliet, one woman operation. You're new. I wondered when you would come over. How are you enjoying Hoppington?'

'Nice to meet you, Juliet, I'm Moira. I haven't seen much of Hoppington yet, but I enjoy the peacefulness and wide-open spaces.'

'Plenty of that around here!' She guffawed. Then the question I knew would come, 'What made a city lady like you move out our way? Mind you we could use a lawyer like you around these parts. Stanley Casey is getting too old for the matters arising these days. He's been a gem sorting out property matters, inheritances and the like, but the winds of change have wafted into our little town. We need new blood in that department.'

'I was looking for a quieter lifestyle, away from the treadmill of the justice department.'

'You're only young yet, or have you retired from the legal business?'

Two minutes in and Juliet was hammer mouth, digging up all she could. She made Jetson a saint.

'I don't know what my plans are yet. I'm here for quiet time, that's all.'

What a relief when she understood.

'I'll let you enjoy your breakfast then. Nice to have you here, Moira.'

I felt like the wicked witch of the west for brushing her off. I was not ready to break the seal on my life for Hoppington's scrutiny.

A long-haired young man entered the cafe. He nodded at Juliet and sat at the opposite end of my table. Not a word passed between him and Juliet. She brought him coffee and two fried eggs. I noticed her touch him on the shoulder and walk away. From the garrulous to the silent in a matter of minutes. I found my legal brain contemplating their relationship. Lovers? He looked too young, but who am I to judge, perhaps brother or son? I stopped my wild thoughts as he looked my way as if he had picked up my thoughts. He nodded when our eyes met. His unsmiling face blitzed a shiver through me. I managed a smile, and a 'good morning,' to which he nodded again from behind his coffee cup. Such encounters never happened in the city. Each person hurried through life, blinkers on, chasing the rainbow of personal success. This young man intended to make a cold connection with me this morning.

I sat around for another ten minutes, skimming through the community newspaper. A birth was announced between the butcher's daughter and the baker's son. A baby boy. A gift bag of cookies was on offer to all customers at the bakery this week to celebrate the birth of baby Joshua. What a lovely sense of community. The rest included advertisements on cattle for sale, a tractor, and a range of other farming equipment. It was refreshing not to have crime in my face on every page as vital city news. An hour and a half at the cafe was all I could handle today. Juliet reiterated how glad she was to have met me and hoped to see more of me. A nod was all she got. No promises, no commitments. I left that behind. The scones looked divine, I grabbed two and strolled back to Dorset Lane. Research on surrounding areas was the plan for my afternoon. My unused car, except for an occasional start and quick rev had to hit the road again.

Dorset Lane was as silent as when I left it a few hours ago. I peered over at number 40 as I opened my front door. The stranger was not outdoors. Perhaps the person went off to work. Now that I had stepped back from my crazy work schedule, I found myself people-watching. I busied myself preparing dinner, a vegetable pasta dinner would go well with the left-over roast chicken in the freezer. I lapsed into laziness and had a raisin toast dinner a few nights in a row. In the middle of preparing my pasta dish, I realised I had no garlic. At 5:30 pm I dashed off to Jetson's grocery store. Starlit eyes greeted me with a toothy grin from behind the counter.

'Ms Moira, good to see you again.'

'Hello Jetson, likewise. Do you have garlic?'

'It's in the fridge, over to your left, that's as fresh as it gets.'

'That's perfect.' I took a pack of cleaned garlic, spring onion and a tiny bunch of coriander.

Jetson beamed up at me, 'What are you cooking tonight? A curry?'

'Pasta. I love it garlicky and herby,' I laughed.

'Sounds good. Have you explored a bit more of our wee town?'

'Yes, I met Juliet earlier today. I had breakfast at her place.'

'Good. But be warned, Juliet is known as the town gossip, so if it's privacy you're after, and I think it is—don't go telling her anything you don't want universally known.' He laughed like a boy who had just shared a girl's secret.

'Thank you for the warning. I'll be sure to heed that. You seem to know me well, already.'

'Generally, nobody will bother you around here, but curiosity for fresh news makes people do strange things, you know.'

'Now about that spring dance, I believe you are selling tickets.'

'I sure am. Glad to hear you've decided to attend. How many tickets do you want?'

'One, please.'

'Not taking a partner along?'

'I don't have one to take.'

'I see. How about you go with me?'

At first, I thought he was kidding, until I saw how deadly serious he was.

'I'd love to go with you, Jetson. That's settled. How much do I owe you for the tickets?'

'It's on me Moira, May I call you Moira? You do know I don't dance much.'

He wheeled himself out from behind the counter. His lower torso was that of an infant.

'Neither do I. We can have an evening together

watching everyone else dance. I owe you for the ticket, or I won't attend.'

'A man at my age never lets a lady pay for her dance ticket. My mama would turn in her grave if she knew I succumbed to modern values!'

We laughed and that was settled. I had garlic, coriander, and a charming date for the spring dance by the time I left Jetson's store.

Back at Dorset Lane, my neighbour at number 40 was reading a book in the yard. The person made no eye contact which disappointed me. One day he, I assumed it was a man, might come over to say hello. I was intrigued by this stranger. What was he reading? Did he live alone?

Tuesday evening seemed a good enough reason for a Chardonnay with dinner and a movie. The spring dance with Jetson would be interesting. It was two weeks away, and I would have to arrange a get-to-know-each-other meet-up before that. He worked seven days a week in the grocery store, so I would have to invite him over one evening before the dance.

I tossed aside watching a movie and decided to read instead.

It was 1:30 am when my eyes opened. The reading lamp was on, and my book lay open on my chest. Two glasses of Chardonnay made me drowsy. My throat had a dry, cracked feel. I might have fallen asleep with my mouth open. A hideous sight I would have been to anyone, even those who had one too many drinks. I stretched my foot on the floor searching for my slippers. A glass of chilled water would soothe that cracked feeling. My feet failed to find my slippers, I walked barefoot to the kitchen. The house was in darkness. I would have to leave the passage light on at night. In my city apartment, streetlights on the front-facing end bathed this area in light for a quick dash to the bath-room or kitchen in the middle of the night. Here, the inky darkness was impenetrable. I felt my way along the dining room chairs and reached for the kitchen light switch, and gasped when I felt something furry against my foot. The kitchen light shone on my bedroom slippers. Could I have been that tipsy to have left my slippers at the kitchen door-way? I could not hold down more than one drink, unlike my attorney peers at Vandruit-in-Law. I made work drinks stretch to avoid being topped up by some overzealous drunk colleague. Tonight, was a reminder to get my act into gear on not drinking more than one glass, alone or not alone. I tossed down a glass of iced water and headed back to bed. This time I left the passage light on and placed my slippers close to the bed.

I lay awake, unable to focus on my reading. Then the thinking hours returned to make me restless.

The police interrogation over Fabian's disappearance claimed my thoughts.

'What are you withholding Ms Barker? You were the last person to see Fabian Costello the night he disappeared. Did he stop to say goodnight to you before he left, or did he say anything else?'

'I did not see him, as I told the first officer. Fabian buzzed me to let me know he was vacating the building as he was exhausted. He told me not to stay in too late, alone.'

'Did he sound anxious? Was there any reason why he was particularly exhausted?'

'Staff worked around the clock. It was expected. Every-body complained about exhaustion.'

'Everybody, such as... give me a few names.'

'I can't pinpoint one person. It was the overall complaint.'

'Fabian would have had privileges as a partner in the firm, am I correct?'

'I don't know.'

'As a family member, what was his relationship like with Mr Vandruit?'

'I can't answer that. I don't know.'

'Ms Barker, is it that you don't know or won't divulge what you know because of your allegiance to your boss?'

These sessions went on every few days, then once a week, and the gap between each widened as Fabian's disappearance faded—the media lost interest as did the investigating officers until an anonymous letter arrived a year later at police headquarters.

The actual details of the letter were never disclosed but hints pointed at Vandruit-in-Law as having a hand in Fabian's mysterious disappearance. Fabian's luxury apartment on the east end waterfront district showed no evidence of a planned trip or a hasty departure. Fabian's weekly grocery order kept rolling. His bank accounts had no recent activity. The letter resulted in a full investigation of Vandruit-in-Law. My stress levels hit the roof. I was hauled through a lie detector test and asked the same questions a year after declaring Fabian's disappearance a cold case. This time I asked questions.

'Am I listed in the apparent anonymous letter as a person of interest?'

The senior officer studied my face with a curled lip that drooped to his large, wobbly, unshaven chin. As politicians do, he answered my question with a question.

'Do you believe you are mentioned in the said letter?'

Believe? What an odd thing to say.

'Not at all. I'm trying to make sense of why I'm being questioned again.'

'Every staff member is being questioned. Time can alter perceptions of the truth. As a legal eagle, you know that.'

This cat-and-mouse game made me nauseous.

'How about letting me get back to my legal eagle work without being made to feel like I'm the criminal.'

'Is that how you feel? Why is that Ms Barker?'

I fell into the trap of making it seem that I was hiding something.

'Your line of questioning suggests I am,' I sighed, 'will that be all then.'

'For now, yes.' The officer looked down at his folder, dismissing me with a wave of his hand.

This dragged on for two weeks until the day Vandruit senior was handcuffed and taken to the station. He was officially charged for withholding evidence regarding an argument he had with Fabian. The anonymous scribe must have been a staffer to share this piece of information.

Then the court summons arrived. I was ordered to give evidence of what I saw or knew about Fabian's disagreements with his father-in-law. A little voice whispered in my head, 'What about being threatened by Vandruit senior to show my allegiance to the firm.' As soon as my part of the hearing was over, I packed up and made my way to Hoppington. Vandruit was held in custody for claiming no involvement even though surveillance footage at his upmarket cove mansion revealed Fabian arriving, with no evidence of him leaving his father-in-law's home. The footage twenty minutes into Fabian's arrival was all there was.

The rest was erased.

***

HERE I WAS PHYSICALLY free from Vandruit-in-Law but chained by memories and nightmares. The spring dance was my priority. I made it a priority to diffuse my persistent thoughts of a time I wanted to forget.

I went over to the little boutique Jetson suggested. Tilly Evans ran a dress shop from her garage. She was a slip of a woman in her sixties. I towered over her when she answered the door.

'Hello dear, you must be Moira. Jetson told me you would come over. How's Hoppington treating you, good, I hope?'

'Lovely to meet you, Tilly. Hoppington is filled with kind folk and I'm enjoying being here.'

'Aww, that's good to know, Moira. I was born and raised here, so I know nowhere else. I'll be buried here too,' she laughed with a gusto I did not expect from such a dainty woman.

As I had anticipated she knew I was going to the dance with Jetson and in need of a dress.

'Let's see what we have for you. My latest arrivals have not been unpacked yet, so if you don't mind coming over to the back of the store, you can have a look through the boxes.'

'Great, I'll start there, thank you, Tilly.'

She pottered at the front of the store, as I browsed through the first box of the latest arrivals. Halfway into the box, I found the perfect dress. A pale blue strapless piece. It was simple yet elegant. A pair of pearl strappy sandals would finish off the ensemble with an understated style.

'Found anything, dear? I heard your excitement. What is it?' Tilly giggled this time.

'Look at this gorgeous blue dress, I'm settling on this.'

'Are you sure? It is lovely, but there are heaps more in the other four boxes.'

'I love this simple style. It's so me, I think.'

'That colour is perfect against your dark skin. What a gorgeous complexion you have.'

'From my father, I believe,' the minute I said it, I regretted it.

'That's lovely, Moira.'

Phew, no questions asked!

Tilly invited me for a cup of tea, but I was quick to decline, saying I had some work to do.

'Ah yes, you must be busy as an attorney.'

Silence was my ally. I smiled, 'What do I owe you for the dress? You haven't tagged these pieces yet.'

'You don't have to pay me now, anytime is fine by me.'

'I prefer to pay now. My city instinct I suppose. I'll wait while you work out the price.'

Tilly flipped through her catalogue and returned.

'$100, dear. Hope that's fair.'

'Generous is more like it! How about I give you $150.'

'No, dear. $100 is the price I'll put on the tags.'

I could not argue with that. I grabbed my bargain and headed back to Dorset Lane.

My neighbour at number 40 was out on the back veranda. Head and shoulders stooped under the wide-brimmed hat.

I tried on my new blue dress. It was a tad baggy around the bust. My darning or sewing skills were zero. I called Tilly to ask if she could nip and tuck it for me.

'I just sell them, dear, can't sew to save my life, I'm afraid. I could suggest Mrs Hutchins on Dorset Lane. She's the first house at the top. She's a bit hard of hearing but an excellent tailor. Try her. Stroll over in the morning. She naps in the afternoon. Tell her I sent you over. Let me know how you go.'

'Thank you, Tilly. You've been a great help.'

'Glad to be of assistance. Pop over any time for a cup of tea.'

Tilly was lovely, but I was nervous about questions about my family background. Thankfully Mrs Hutchins was hard of hearing.

With that settled, I poured myself a gin and tonic turned to the melodies of Earl Klugh and toyed with the idea of getting a dog. It had crossed my mind many times, but each time I halted the thought of whether it would be fair to get a dog if I was planning on being on the move as the whim arose. Overthinking is what Harriet said was my weakness that prevented risk-taking. She sure was right about that. Harriet dared to be different. She said, 'If you don't test your limits how will you ever know what you can or can't do, just yet? It's like being a champion athlete. They were not born great, but they sure as hell gave it a try, a damn hard try at that too!' She added the 'just yet' to convince me that anything was possible with persistence. How I missed her. I'm not sure what she would think if she knew I had moved to her old hometown. She withheld memories of the sadness in her early life. I pondered whether Mrs Hutchins, the tailor, would remember my mother. I wanted to know what the old townsfolk thought of my mother, running off alone with a full belly of me. If anything, I owed it to her to exorcise my demons. 'Hold that head of yours up high, Moira, you hear. You came into this world because your mama wanted you, and I sure as hell raised you in no charity. You don't forget that now.' She was hard and compassionate. Nobody she knew would be without a warm plate any day of the year. She would rather go with an empty belly than watch someone go hungry.

There was history here in Hoppington and I needed to lift the lid that Harriet shut. Whether I wanted to know who my father was, is another question I had to mull over. I had no interest in knowing, but now, this town was pulling me in, inch by inch. I wafted off to sleep, restless with that thought.

I woke with a startle when I heard a sound in the back-yard. My curtains were wide open and the dim lampposts on Dorset Lane cast billowing shadows across my couch. I picked up my mobile phone off the coffee table, it was 1:30 am. I had fallen asleep for almost six hours. I rose to shut the lounge curtains and caught sight of the lit yard at number 40. My unknown neighbour was hanging washing on the line at this hour. I pulled away from the window when the figure looked up. Pants, shirts, socks, and a towel floated up and down in the wind. I drew the curtains and went to the kitchen to make a sandwich. The gin and tonic I had before dinner lulled me off. I heard the sound in the backyard again. I opened the kitchen door and a cat scuttled away as lithe as a gentle breeze. I had never considered safety to be an issue in this little rural town. I was at the furthest end of Dorset Lane but felt no threat being alone here. The city created anxiety, drawn from the suspicion that strangers were not to be trusted. What an inverted world if safety is always a priority. I had a triple-bolted front door and armed windows in a skyscraper block and I was two floors from the top! It's not like I housed the Crown Jewels. My computer and legal files were the most important wares in my home. Hoppington opened head-space on values and human relationships. Vandruit-in-Law purported to uphold unbreakable values as the bedrock of the firm and did a good job of presenting itself as such until Fabian disappeared. I found myself thinking about Fabian more often than I wanted to. I suppose he was the only authentic person in the firm. When he spoke to you, he saw you. His interactions were sparse after his wife died. He was reclusive, only ever engaging in legal matters when it was necessary.

I jumped into bed around 3 am after setting my alarm for 7 am. I had to see Mrs Hutchins in the morning, Tilly made a point of recommending the morning as the best time to see her. I had to get some groceries from Jetson so I decided breakfast at Juliet's would make it a full day of being a local.

***

MRS HUTCHINS WAS a woman of advanced years with no obvious physical limitations except as Tilly said, she was hard of hearing. Her smile, as she opened the door, widened when I told her Tilly sent me to her for some alteration work on a dress. The magnetism of her presence placed a perpetual smile on my face as I absorbed the light of her beautiful aura.

'Come in dearie, please speak up, you're very soft. How are you, Moira?'

'Good, good thank you, Mrs Hutchins. Thank you for seeing me at such short notice.'

'I have all the time in the world, not much happens here except for the Spring Ball. Come let's have a look at your dress. Tilly has some lovely dresses, doesn't she?'

'She sure does. I know I'll be going back to her soon for more dresses.'

'She'll love that. You could become a model for her. You are a beautiful young lady. Are you here alone in Hoppington?'

Nobody had ever referred to me as beautiful save for dear Harriet. Mrs Hutchins was sadly mistaken with her rather thick lens glasses.

'A model! I laughed. I'm too old for that.'

Don't judge yourself, my dear, you are too hard on yourself. See what the world sees of you.'

I was gobsmacked that a stranger to my life and personality summed up my poor self-regard with such accuracy.

'You are too kind for saying so, Mrs Hutchins.'

'There you did it again.'

I laughed and she squeezed my arm like a loving grandmother. In that moment I missed Harriet even more. She was all the family I had or knew.

Mrs Hutchins insisted I stay for lunch, and I obliged. There was a wonderful warmth that encircled her that made me want to stay longer. It was during this first meeting with her that I asked if she knew an old resident, Harriet... I was careful not to mention she was my mother.

'Aye, I remember her well, pretty young thing, very bright at school. Sadly, she got mixed up with the wrong fella and left town. Never heard from her again. Do you know Harriet?'

'No, I don't, someone I worked with told me about her when she knew I was moving to Hoppington.'

'Small world indeed. I would love to know what became of her. If you can get her phone number, I would love a chat. You know, I was Harriet's teacher.'

My chest heaved. Here was someone, from my mother's

past, who knew her well. The desire to know more pulsated in my head, but I had to leave that shut, for now.

'I will.' The lie made me hot and edgy.

'Harriet's old beau died last year. He left after she did but returned a year later and never left again. Married and settled here. His wife is still alive. She's Juliet's older sister. Have you met Juliet from the coffee shop?'

Small world indeed. The circle was closing around me, making me uncomfortable.

'Yes, I've met Juliet. I was planning on going over after I saw you, but you kindly invited me to lunch.'

'It's good to have your company, Moira. Us old folk get a bit lonely sometimes.'

I wanted to tell her that we younger folk get lonely often.

A chat about the Dorset Lane neighbours was a good idea. Mrs Hutchins was the town oracle and long-standing resident of Dorset Lane. All I had to ask was how long has the Lane neighbourhood been the same before my arrival.

'We've all grown up here, so we know each other like family. The only newer resident on Dorset Lane is the gentleman at number 40, I don't even know his name. The quiet, distant type. Must be a writer I think, he's always reading. I hear he's quite polite when locals see him shopping at Jetson's store.'

'How interesting, I've seen somebody in the yard, now I know it's a man.'

'Don't you go getting any ideas now,' Mrs Hutchins laughed, 'we hope you will stay on and not run off as Harriet did.'

Her words haunted me for quite some time that day. I wanted to ask her more about what she remembered about

Harriet but feared my emotions would reveal my family history.

I headed over to Jetson's supermarket lost in thoughts and visions of what Harriet's life was like as a child in Hoppington. Jetson was not at his counter. I heard his voice in the back office. He seemed to be arguing with someone on the telephone.

'I cannot do that; you need to get out there and make a life for yourself.'

He must have heard me in the front of the store because he ended his call abruptly.

'Moira, lovely to see you,' he was flushed and a little out of breath.

'Hi Jetson, sorry, I was about to leave when I did not see you at the counter.'

'There's a bell in front that you can ring if I'm not at the counter. I slip to the back sometimes for the bathroom or to make myself a quick cuppa.'

'That's ok, I'll just wait, rather than hurry you to finish whatever you're doing.'

He laughed that schoolboy laugh 'Not much hurrying around for me.'

'I dropped by for some canned goods, and to tell you I'm all set for the dance. How about you?'

'My black tux is fresh and ready to go. Thank you for accepting my invitation to the dance. It will be a great evening where you will meet all the townsfolk.'

'I look forward to that Jetson. Now, will you accept a dinner invitation at my place any day of your choice?'

'That's lovely, but you don't have to do that.'

'How about I insist you come over for dinner,' I smiled.

'Now a man should never turn down a lovely lady like

yourself. Perhaps Saturday evening will suit me, how about you?'

'Great! Any day is good for me. That's settled. How about this Saturday?'

'Wonderful! Is that why you're stocking up on canned goods.' Jetson had a cheeky twinkle in his eye.

'You shall have to wait and see.'

I left Jetson feeling a lot lighter after Mrs Hutchins shared a memory of Harriet in Hoppington. I looked forward to having Jetson dine in my home, and I planned to cook my mother's favourite Sunday pot roast with gravy which was the highlight of my week. There were a few things that needed to be arranged before the dinner. Cleaning up the place, and a visit to the butcher for his best leg of lamb was number one on my to-do list.

Saturday evening arrived a lot quicker in this laid-back haven than I had anticipated. A bottle of red was out on the dining room sideboard with two glasses ready to go. Rosemary-infused roast lamb permeated my home. Roast potatoes and tenderly roasted vegetables made a great accompaniment to the roast. Mama's speciality. I selected a Beethoven playlist for the evening. Jetson was still relatively unknown to me and inviting someone to my home under such conditions was a first.

I strolled into the veranda to wait for Jetson. A black sedan eased down Dorset Lane and stopped outside number 40. The familiar stranger from number 40 walked up to the sedan, and much to my surprise, Jetson's head and arm popped out the window to shake the stranger's hand. Jetson handed over a small package, they chatted briefly, and the stranger walked back to his gate. I pulled back inside the house and decided to wait indoors for Jetson. Through the lounge room windows, I observed

Jetson pull up in front of my house and the stranger watched him get out before he walked into his house.

I met Jetson out on the veranda. It was a balmy evening. He looked tired but held onto his charming smile and cheery greeting.

'Moira, I made it! Thank you so much for inviting me over. I have not been out anywhere except to the yearly spring dance, but this year I have the loveliest lady I know to accompany me.'

'You are such a charmer, Jetson! You must have a bevy of beauties breaking down your door.'

'Too kind, that's what you are, come on show me in, I smell something heavenly cooking in there.'

I laughed at his determination to be jovial. He said nothing about stopping at number 40 Dorset Lane and I pondered whether I should tell him I saw him drive over and chat with someone. Perhaps later after dinner was a better idea.

It was lovely to have company that posed no risk to my anxiety. We chatted over a glass of wine, and Jetson shared how he met his wife, Bella on a trip to San Francisco. She was a guest at a friend's wedding, and they felt a mutual attraction from the first dance.

'It was a magical time. We spent forty-five glorious years together, travelling during the years when I had a manager run the supermarket for me. After Bella passed, I threw myself into my work, it helped the grieving.' He looked at me with a wistful eye and was silent for a while.

'What a blessing to have a soulmate to share beautiful years.'

'I keep reminding myself how lucky I was to have met Bella. With no children, all she left me with are memories to help me pull through each day. I don't mean to intrude, but do you have a fella in the city or are you footloose and fancy-free?'

We both laughed and on that last note I poured us another glass of wine and we tucked into the roast, gravy, and vegetables.

'No fella in the city and none in the offing. I prefer it that way.'

Jetson nodded.

'Like you, I spent a great deal of my life mourning my mother's passing.'

'I'm so sorry to have opened a wound for you, you don't have to say anything more if it makes you sad.'

'I miss her, I too threw myself into my work and never bothered with seeking a relationship. I never knew my father as I was raised by a single mother. She was the best parent any child could have had.'

Jetson listened and nodded, never stopping me to probe for more information. A third glass of wine set my tongue loose. I felt so comfortable around him that I let down my guard.

'You might know my mother if you've been in Hoppington all your life.'

He raised his eyes and looked at me, the familiar twinkle I got used to, dulled. I knew his mind was racing, and then I felt a surge of emotions whip through my body when he said, 'You must be Harriet's daughter, Harriet Parkes' daughter.' He reached across the table and squeezed my hand.

My mother registered me under her grandma Ruby's maiden name, Barker, to protect my identity from my unknown father.

'Yes, I am,' is all I could utter before the floodgates opened.

Jetson wheeled himself over to me, told me to sit on the couch and moved himself to the seat beside me. He cradled my face and placed my head on his shoulder and let me weep like a child.

'You have held this in for a long time. You have nothing to be afraid of or ashamed of. Harriet was the darling of Hoppington. We were devastated when she left, never to return. I am so happy you returned to her childhood home-town. It took great courage to do that.'

We sat on the couch for two hours until Jetson offered to make us a coffee if I showed him where things were in my tiny kitchen. I jumped up and insisted on making the coffee.

At midnight I waved Jetson goodbye from the veranda and saw my neighbour at number 40 look up at me, and then walk back inside the house. My heart raced.

Had he been watching me while I watched him?

Why?

I felt uneasy, drew the curtains, turned off the lounge lights and went to the kitchen to tidy up. I jumped out of my skin when my mobile phone rang. It was Jetson checking if I was ok. For the first time in my life, after Harriet passed, someone cared if I was ok. Now that's special in my book!

***

THE DAY of the spring dance arrived.

Barber Ned, hairdresser et al, booked me in for a 4 pm appointment. My hair was glossy and bobbed around making me feel like I had stepped out on a catwalk in Milan. What an amazing feeling. Ned smiled at my obvious approval of his transformation from dull to sheer shine and a huge lift to the former flatness.

'Well, I think, as a beautiful out-of-towner you will be the belle of the spring ball, Ms Moira.'

'You're too kind, Ned. I'm no out-of-towner. Hoppington is home to my soul.'

Ned glowed as much as my freshly coiffed hair. My conversation with Jetson on what the town thought of Harriet was my acceptance that this was indeed home.

I was nervous about meeting more townsfolk but with Jetson by my side, I knew I would be more than fine. He arrived promptly at 7 pm with a yellow rose in hand, refusing that I meet him at his place. A traditionalist, a proper gentleman in every way. What a refreshing difference to my experience at Vandruit-in-Law.

'Thank you, Jetson, for everything.'

'Everything? We haven't even started the evening yet, my dear,' he laughed and nudged my arm. I felt safe and respected. In some uncanny way, what he said about my mother made him a good man in my book.

I had not been to a dance since junior high, I felt young and vibrant again, watching happy couples enter the dance hall. The wonderful sounds of Marvin Gaye floated out to greet the night. Jetson looked dapper in his tuxedo; his sparse hair gelled back. I knew this night and the anticipation of it had lifted the years off him.

'I'll fill you in on who's who as the night progresses.'

'Great, I have just skimmed the surface of the population at Hoppington'

'There are not many more but a few you should know for services or friendships you will need.'

'Friendships' Jetson? Whatever for when I have you.'

He laughed the laugh I was growing to love hearing. It was warm, genuine, and cheeky.

'Now you're too kind, but I'll take that!'

The music flowed, bodies swayed, and introductions were aplenty. My eyes searched for a resemblance to my unknown neighbour at number 40 Dorset Lane. Nobody fitted the physical demeanour of the person I saw across from my cottage.

'Does everyone in Hoppington attend the spring dance?'

'Most do, except the infirm, I suppose.'

'I was wondering whether my neighbour from 40 Dorset Lane was here tonight?'

Jetson gave me the same measured, corner-eyed look when he told me he knew Harriet.

'No, he's not here tonight. Not much of a socialite I'm afraid.'

Now I was silent, not sure if it would be an intrusion to ask why. Jetson had a connection to my neighbour which was not my business.

'Ah, I see. I find him interesting in his reclusiveness. I was a tad perturbed when I first noticed him. My city fear crept in with a touch of the legal profiling of hermit-like persons, I think. Not a fair judgement.'

Jetson looked uncomfortable. His usual casual, relaxed manner, was gone. Then he looked at me with what I perceived as sadness in his eyes.

'Let's go outdoors for some air, is that ok, dear?'

'I was just about to suggest that.' I hated my white lie but was relieved to see him relax again.

'It's time you called me Jet, like everybody else.' His warm smile returned.

It was a beautiful starry night. A cool breeze was welcome outside the packed dance hall.

'Moira, my dear. Do you mind if I say you look so much like Harriet? She would have been singing here tonight, in the old days. She drew people to the dance with her beautiful voice.'

'That has warmed my heart, I hope in the days ahead, if you don't mind, that you will share more of your memories of her.'

'It will be an honour and privilege to do so. I have something to tell you.'

I expected to hear more about Harriet and tensed in anticipation of what appeared to be a forthcoming revelation from Jetson.

'It does not feel right not to be honest with you, Moira. You have opened your heart to me, and I appreciate your trust.

My stomach was in a knot.

'You asked about your neighbour at number 40. He's my son from a teenage relationship. His mother, too, left town to have him, and I never heard from her again until he returned to Hoppington. He has a bad leg from an injury, he says. Much of his life is off-limits to me. He is loving and kind but bears an intense sadness he won't share. I know nothing about his life before he arrived in Hoppington, but I'm grateful he's here. There's nothing worse than knowing you are a parent to a child you have never met.'

Every word Jetson uttered struck a chord deep within me. He needed to talk, and I needed to hear what he said.

'I would love to introduce him to you. You are also a private person. That's what struck me about you on the first day you came to the supermarket. But lots rest on whether he will be open to meeting you.'

'It would be good to meet your son. Let's see how it goes once you suggest it to him.'

'Thank you for listening, Moira.'

I bent over and put my arms around Jetson, A gentle hug was enough to let him know I understood.

We went back into the dance hall, lighter after deepening our connection.

Jetson drove me home around 11:30 pm.

'I hope you had a wonderful night, Moira. I sure did, and I'm so glad you're here in Hoppington. Have a good night's rest. I'll go over to tell Fabian about my evening. He'll be up reading.'

My heart skipped a beat. Was this why the stranger at number 40 Dorset Lane caught my attention? Fabian crouched over his desk at the firm just as my unknown neighbour did over his book. Visions of Fabian's face from memory revealed a younger Jetson.

He watched me as I watched him.

CROSSINGS

To be without family is the tragedy of birth. To relinquish family is the unnaturalness of a misled mind and a heart that never felt. To find family in friendships is the saviour to wholesome survival.

CROSSINGS

How I ended up in an orphanage with a house mother and house father—yes that is what we called our guardian parents, will be my endless search. I often wondered about my genes that left me with a head of curly dark brown hair, pixie ears and pale freckled skin. I was the tallest girl for my age at school and the orphanage.

Eighteen marked my get-out-of-jail birthday card. The orphanage was never my jail, but rather my safe place with my large family, eight girls and six boys. I grew up here. I knew nothing else but the dark blue, uncarpeted floors, the smell of disinfectant in the corridors, and single beds lined up four or six per narrow room with windows so high there was no view of the outside. Sunlight penetrated the unreachable windows to warm the austerity of faded blue flooring, repainted many times over, highlighting yellowing, once-white walls.

When my house mother and house father asked to see me in private the night before I turned eighteen—I had no idea that my life would change forever. I was the eldest orphan in the complex of six cottages. We were the envy of the other five cottages because Grace and Daniel, my house parents, were the best any child could wish for. Grace had the perfect name. It said everything about her kindness, which shone from her heart to her soft eyes. Daniel, some of the boys called him Danny Dad, was our very own Santa Claus. He was gargantuan, with a beard that glistened down his chest. Gentlefolk. An orphan's dream parents.

I arrived in the common room with the same faded blue floors and yellowing once-white walls, except that Grace had a vase of wilting wildflowers on the main table. I expected to hear that a grand eighteenth birthday party was planned. Sunshine Shelter was the only home I knew. Now that is an unfortunate name, the sunshine bit I liked, but 'shelter' sounded like a parking lot for abandoned vehicles or a place for unwanted and forgotten pets. Grace and Daniel never made me, or any of my peers, feel unwanted or forgotten.

'Well, well, well! Who do we have here? Miss eighteen-year-old herself!'

Daniel had a way of babying everyone, including Grace. He teased, laughed and questioned, but a shadow behind his light hazel eyes warned me that this was not a celebratory meeting. Grace was unusually quiet. She met my gaze when I turned from Daniel's forced jubilance to her wide-staring eyes.

'Thank you, but give me a break, let me be seventeen for a few more hours!' I laughed but heard my strange louder than was usual echoey voice ask, 'Is everything ok?'

Both piped in, one loud, the other soft, 'No...not really.'

'What is it? Just tell me. Have I done something I should not have done? You both are so awkward. I've never seen you this way before.'

Daniel cleared his throat, twirled the ends of his silvery-red beard, and looked at Grace. She nodded.

'You could never do anything wrong in our eyes, Ruby. The board has a new ruling. We have been told that you must leave as soon as you find accommodation. Sunshine Shelter is now only for under eighteen-year-olds. We are so sorry, Ruby, it's not what we want. This was thrust upon us last week. We have been struggling with how we were going to say this to you.'

I looked at Grace, her mouth was moving but all I heard was a slow tear-laden unclear sound.

'Ssssooorrrry...'

'How soon do I have to be out?'

'The board said they would allow two weeks. I will help you look for accommodation,' Grace said, her eyes glistening.

'My sister has a spare room in her place if you can't find anything suitable right away,' Daniel whispered, averting his eyes from me.

'Thank you, Daniel, may I call you Daniel now, I'm about to make my way in the world alone?'

He coughed and nodded. I'm not sure if he was upset that I seemed to be abandoning respect for him after all these years. I arrived here at two weeks old, and eighteen wonderful years is what I had. This was my safe place, my home. The only family I knew. Now I was being kicked out. Dispensed with. Deep down I knew a day would come when I would have to leave, but not this soon. Rules are rules, I get that. You must admit, it is a cruel rule. Are children kicked out of their biological family homes at eighteen? I had no idea of the world outside Sunshine Shelter. Besides, it was not like the place was bursting at the seams with too many kids needing a bed!

That evening marked my entrance into the adult world, my third crossing, the journey to finding myself. The sunshine I felt here all these years left my world that day.

***

MY FIRST FEW days of school life were the early beginnings of my awareness that I was different. Everybody had an elaborate packed lunch that tickled my nostrils with longing. Some parents brought in a piping hot meal for their children. I had a cheese sandwich and a bottle of apple juice every Monday. An egg and mayo sandwich on Tuesdays with another bottle of apple juice, and Wednesday was peanut butter and jam day with a blue milkshake. Thursday and Friday were fish finger sandwiches loaded with tomato sauce, and a banana milkshake to wash down the dryness of bread and crumbed fish slapped together between two slices of near mouldy bread. I never complained. Grace and Daniel did not prepare school lunches, they arrived at our house door from the orphanage's main kitchen. A few cruel kids peered into my lunch box during our meal breaks making puking sounds, but I never told Daniel and Grace how I felt. Yeah, I was made to feel my difference by the lunch I ate at school.

During my primary school days, I had one friend, Greta, a refugee who escaped the Bosnian war with her single mother. Greta clung to me as I to her. I helped her with English, and she paid me in loyal friendship. She had the most beautiful singing voice with depth and height that I had never heard before. She was stunning, with no idea that she was a portrait of perfection. Her shiny black hair, peachy skin, dark brown eyes and smile always caught the admiring glances of all who met her.

Her mother had a rush of shiny, black hair cascading down her back. Her dangly hoop earrings, blue eyeshadow and red lips made her a movie star to me. She rolled her r's and only ever called me 'darrrrling.' She saw me and made me feel special.

When Greta invited me to spend a Saturday afternoon at her mum's one-bedroom apartment, Daniel told me I could not visit until they had met Greta's mother. My much-anticipated visit was on hold for a few months until I asked again if I could go to Greta and her mother.

'We should have Greta and her mum over for a meal, after which we hope to be invited to their home before you have permission to visit on your own. Does that sound fair, Ruby?' Grace was gentle, and her offering seemed reasonable.

Greta must be like the father she had never met. She was shy and quiet when she was not singing. Her mother was a social butterfly. The day they came to Sunshine Shelter for dinner, our cottage turned into a carnival site. Greta's mother's leopard print catsuit, dangly hoop earrings that almost touched her shoulders, and bright pink pouty lips created a sight never seen at the orphanage. She cooed over my peers, calling all 'darrrrling,' including Daniel—he enjoyed every moment, smiling coyly under his Santa Claus beard. His eyes never hid his emotions!

The kids from the other cottages gathered to see what caused the laughter and merriment that floated out from our place. Alas, their house parents reined them in and shut their cottage doors.

We had a lavish meal of roast chicken and vegetables and a mango cheesecake dessert—it felt like Christmas. Grace and Daniel relaxed around Greta's mum, and we visited their home two weeks later. The green light was up after that visit. I could see Greta one Saturday afternoon each month. Greta's tiny home became my second home, a ticket to a few hours of feeling normal.

The time we spent together outside school sealed our friendship. I had to tell Greta I received the order of the boot from Sunshine Shelter. It was not my house parents' fault that I received my marching orders. Turning eighteen was my curse. That I fully understood. My eyebrows had never been tidied, and my fingernails were short and unvarnished. My hair needed a trim, but I learned to pull it up and away from my face, adding to my austere look.

**

MY FIRST LIFE crossing was my birth, of course, for which I have no memory. My second crossing was my arrival at Daniel's and Grace's cottage—that draws another blank on how I got there—nothing stored in the memory bank.

Now at this third crossing, I felt homeless for the first time, a wanderer with no biological connections and a future that seemed as grey as the sky on the morning I left Sunshine Shelter. I had to go it alone, so I declined Greta's offer to park off at her mother's flat until I knew what my next crossing would be. Instead, I turned up at a women's shelter on the west side of town. It was a place offering no promises of anything other than a bed, shower, breakfast and one other meal a day. The woman in charge, Antoinette Lavazza, seemed nice enough. I saw the comforting kindness in her eyes. When you live as I have, you know that kindness in the eyes of someone is a hopeful sign. You hang onto every act of kindness those eyes promise. I faced many unkind people in my life. They had stony eyes and unmovable faces.

I had to find a job, right? How would I pay for another meal without one? The women's shelter allowed me to stay for three months if I proved I was not sitting on my laurels, and that I was actively seeking work.

It was time to find my way in the world I did not understand. I was unprepared. I felt like a child thrown to the wolves.

***

THE WOMEN'S shelter aided with drafting my résumé and preparing me for an interview. There was not much to add by way of work experience. All I had ever done in my short life was help with chores at the orphanage, and help manage a food stand on fundraising days. The thing is with fifty of us in the shelter, it was a clamber to get an audience with the volunteers who came in to offer employment advice. There was one woman who helped with the résumé and just one who helped with the interview preparation.

To get ahead in the queue, you had to submit a statement on why you should be put ahead of the pack. How would I get there? I was new and single and there were scores of women who had children, were victims of domestic violence and had been homeless for a long time. I gave it a try. I used the facilities at my disposal at the shelter and filled out every job vacancy within a ten-kilometre radius. I wanted to study and needed a job that did not take up too much of my day in useless travelling time.

The first reply was for a waitress position at a local Italian restaurant. I waited forty-eight hours before I responded. Somewhere I read that one should sit on a deci-sion for forty-eight hours to know if that's really what you want. I had no option, but I was prepared to wait. Grace instilled never being impulsive and that stuck with me. I missed many opportunities at school by adhering to her rule.

Forty-eight hours later, there was no response from the other sixty positions I had applied for. Who would want to employ someone with no experience, *nix*, fresh out of high school, and no background?

I accepted the waitressing job, and an instantaneous reply urged me to take up the position the next evening. The email stated: to wear black pants, a black shirt, and a black bandana. You are also required to wear your smile!'

Black pants and a shirt, and my smile were not a prob-lem. I had no black bandana and not enough money to buy one. One of the rules at the shelter was to inform Antoinette when a job was secured. Here there was a thirty-day kick-out policy once you acquired a job. The wait-ressing position was from 7 pm to midnight three nights a week.

I popped over to Antoinette's office around 5 pm, just before dinner. Dinner was served at 5:30 pm at the Sunshine Shelter. Must be something to do with living in an institution.

'Hey Ruby, everything okay, girl?' The smile in her voice and the warmth in her eyes gave me hope.

'I have some good news, ma'am.'

'Drop that ma'am business. I'm not the school princi-pal, you know. I hope you don't mind me calling you 'girl.' You are the youngest woman I've ever had in here. Now tell me, Ruby, what's going on in that busy head of yours?'

'I enjoy being the youngest! Call me anything you like.

You have been so kind to me, Antoinette. It's good news, I have secured a part-time position. I start tomorrow.'

'Well, well! That's fast work! I saw you as a determined young thing when you walked in here just four days ago. Good on you, tell me about it.'

'It's not much, just a waitressing job at the Italian restaurant in town. It involves night work.'

'You've never worked before, so how is this a 'not much' job to you? Hear this lesson, and hear it well; gratitude for the grace you have received must not be made light of, you hear that girl?'

'Sorry, I did not mean to sound ungrateful. I'm a little anxious about the pay and whether I will survive, on my own. I want to study and work, and there will be plenty of bills to pay.'

'Cross each thing one day at a time. Get the experience and then work on your goals. You have a month here of free board so save what you can and keep your eye out for other jobs too. You're lucky they did not want to interview you. You must have written a heck of an application for the position. Can I help you with anything? You will have free board for another month when you start your job, so it is expected that you will help around here in some small way. Think you can do that?'

'Thank you for your kind advice. Yes, I will help in any way I can, just ask, please Antoinette. I don't have a black bandana, it's one of the requirements of the dress code, and I don't have the money to get one by tomorrow.'

'Let me see what I can do. I am a mean seamstress if I say so myself so let me put one together. Come over in the morning and we shall work something out. Get over to dinner before the food's finished!'

Antoinette's hearty laugh calmed my worry and, somehow, I knew she would deliver on her promise.

***

Decked in my black attire and matching bandana I bounced with excitement and nervousness to my first shift. This was my fourth life crossing.

Vincente's was abuzz from seven to midnight. My understanding of the word, 'waitressing' was delusional. Here it meant general dogsbody. Whatever needed doing, a waitress was expected to do it! Washing dishes, serving tables and fixing whatever needed mending included just a few requirements of the role. But I'm not complaining. I need the money! I'm desperate! I don't like to hear myself think that, but I cannot run away from that reality.

Rahul, my manager, gave me the once-over. I sensed his displeasure. Was this going to be like my school days again? Being born on the wrong side of *acceptable* made me noticed for all the wrong reasons! Had he just read my résumé? No work experience. Well, paid work experience, I'll concede to, but I did work, and I am adaptable!

'Think you can handle this busy place, Ruby? His eyebrows knitted into an even monobrow.

'I'll learn quickly, and I apologise if I'm not as fast as the rest of the team. In a week you won't know the difference, I guarantee.'

The monobrow stayed in place, but Rahul's eyes darkened.

'Fast and accurate is what we need here at Vincente's. Natalie will show you what's expected.'

I smiled and turned to Natalie who beckoned me to her

side of the restaurant.

'Hey Ruby, so glad you could join us this soon. It is our busiest week! We sure can use the extra hand around here!'

My voice croaked, 'Really? Is it just this time of year?'

'We are always busy, this week we are understaffed. Do you have a commercial driver's permit?'

Natalie was not wasting any time. The small talk ended there.

'I don't drive. I hope I will soon... it's one of my goals.'

She eyed me with suspicion. Most people my age own cars. Natalie did not know my birth history. How could she, neither did I!

'Better get moving on that if you want to be recognised for versatility on the job. You will go places, get my drift?'

'Yes, yes, I do, thank you!'

'Go to the kitchen, two kitchen hands are away. Wash the plates and larger utensils by hand and put the glasses and cutlery in the dishwasher.'

What a slog on my first night. My way into the working world was a life initiation! I washed dishes, kept an eye on empty tables, cleared them and went back to washing. As a novice, I was not allowed, thankfully, to set the tables! Don't get me wrong, I'm not a lazy person, but fear had me worried that I might do something wrong and get fired on the first night. I had no self-confidence, but I promised to educate myself out of this destructive mindset.

Pizza and pasta, my favourite foods, left me with dishes that were not so easy to clean. The cheese and tomato sauce formed black crusts that needed to be chiselled out. I worked with my head down, thankful to have a job. The kitchen bustled and nobody spoke to me. I don't think anybody noticed I was the new girl in the zone. I figured from a few sly glances behind me that the chef was the young man with mousey brown hair with one green streak to the right of his head. He moved like lightning in coordinated ballerina swirls! He said nothing, read the cards pinned on the board above him and danced his way to the fridges and ovens with such grace! I did not expect a young, cool chef, I half expected someone like Daniel, an older and perhaps more rotund person. Not that I have anything against the young man with the green stripe head, at all. I had this vision of old and rotund fixed in my head for some obtuse reason.

The world was unfolding, letting me know I had a lot of catching up to do. Was it the institution I was raised in or was it me? It felt like I had not lived in this world at all after my first night at work.

The aroma in the kitchen made me wish I had eaten more before I came to work. Nobody told me to take a break, least of all have a slice of pizza! I worked the full five hours non-stop. At the end of my shift, when I undid my apron, Natalie was onto me, mop and bucket in hand.

'Please mop up the kitchen floor and help tidy the dining floor before you leave. Remember what I said earlier this evening?' She raised her well-arched eyebrows and glared at me.

I was back in yesteryear, a student living on the fringes of everything!

At 12:45 am I walked back to the shelter. My feet hurt, my back ached, and my clothes were drenched down the front, but I was happy. This was my first day of independence. I earned my first pay, although I had no change jingling in my pocket tonight.

***

Lourdes sat outside her room, smoking. She barely spoke to me in my short time at the shelter but seemed to be up waiting for me. Word got around fast in this joint.

'Got any leftover pizza to share? We heard you are working over at Vincente's.'

'Hi Lourdes, no I'm sorry, I have no pizza. Nobody offered any leftover pizza. It was my first night.'

'You just take leftovers, nobody gonna offer you nothing, you hear that! Learn fast, and take what you can. Push yourself *sista*! I expect something after your next shift.' She stood up, gave me a backward glare, and shut her room door.

Lourdes was in her forties, a chain smoker who bumped cigarettes off the other women.

I felt an old fear creeping back into my life.

I showered and slept like the dead.

I woke to a loud banging on my door. Three women I only knew by sight from the dining hall stood outside with their hands on their hips.

'Hey Ruby, got a moment to help us apply for jobs? You secured one fast. We've been trying for a long time.' The woman doing the talking looked a lot older than Lourdes.

I blinked, rubbed my eyes, and whispered, 'Sure, give me an hour to get ready, I'll meet you in the dining hall.'

'An hour? What do you need to do? From what we hear, you work nights, girl, so why do you need an hour?'

'I'll be there as soon as I can. I'm not sure how much I can help, but I'm willing to give it a try.'

That seemed to have satisfied them as they hurried off to the dining hall. I had to have a word with Antoinette at some point during the morning.

The breakfast room buzzed. Groups of women huddled together in conversation. All eyes turned in my direction when I walked in, my hair still wet from a hurried shower.

I grabbed a banana at the entrance and headed to the continental breakfast table. Antoinette ensured that breakfast was the best meal served at the shelter. Hot breakfasts and cold cuts, warm porridge, and fruits of the season to enjoy with a tiny tub of yoghurt. If Sunshine Shelter was good, Antoinette made this place a high-end resort.

A group of women surrounded my table as I lifted the first spoonful of cereal into my mouth. Now, let me tell you, muesli requires intense mastication, so these ladies had to wait.

All wanted help with their résumés, and all spoke at the same time. I felt faint from the expectation that would become the norm if I stayed here longer than stipulated. Then a voice roared from behind the mob.

'Let the girl have her breakfast! She is under no obligation to help you unless she chooses to. Get back to your tables, please ladies!'

Gabriella, the kitchen assistant who never said much until now, silenced the mob. They grumbled, some under their breaths, others audibly as they returned to their seats.

'You, ok, Ruby?'

'Yes, thank you, Gabriella. Thank you for what you just did.'

'Geez, you are as white as a sheet. Have your breakfast, talk to no one on your way out and head to Antoinette's office. She wants to see you.'

'Thank you, I will.'

My knees rattled like an ancient skeleton as I walked out of the breakfast room. Many sets of eyes followed me. Was I a hero or an enemy now that I had a job?

Antoinette's office door was open. She looked up when she heard my hurried footsteps.

'Shut the door. You look like a hundred demons are after you! Sit down, start at the beginning, and tell me everything. I want names. Think you can do that?'

'Names? Why?'

'Bullying is my pet peeve! We have surveillance around here. I saw Lourdes waiting for you at that ungodly hour, and I heard the skirmish if I can call it that, at breakfast.'

'Lourdes thought I had leftover pizza, and the ladies this morning want me to help them with their résumés and job applications. I'll do the best I can. I start my college studies next week, I'm not sure how much I can help the ladies with their requests.'

Antoinette leaned forward and looked me straight in the eye. The moment felt like the day the principal called me to the office because a kid said I had stolen his pencil case. I was not guilty but felt as though I had done something wrong. This guilt lived inside me. I knew I was not responsible for the things I was accused of doing, during my life, but I cowered and shuffled, and that made me the bad girl.

'We have people appointed to assist the ladies with their job hunt. You do not have to do this. When I asked you to assist around here, I meant with tidying up the place when you had some time, and not on any roster as such.'

'I think the ladies are awestruck that I secured a job after arriving here a few days ago.'

'Put that aside for now, tell me about your first night as a working woman.'

We both giggled with Antoinette punching the air and leaning over with interest in her eyes. After I explained what 'waitressing' entailed at Vincente's, her silence made me awkward. Had I said something arrogant or did I seem too complaining about my first day of work?

Antoinette sucked in her breath, 'It certainly is tough out there and as a newbie, you will be taken advantage of if you don't speak up. What's the worst thing that can happen? More chores? Perhaps. You will not be fired because they already know they have gold in you.'

Nobody had ever said that to me. I did not know how to react.

'What's wrong, nobody praised you before?'

'No.'

'Look up Ruby when you are praised and extend some gratitude. This helpless demeanour will get you nowhere. I grew up on the rough side of the street. It's not easy to rise above that, but you must want a better life with every fibre of your being, or you will forever be on the wrong side of the tracks. Now, look at me.'

I managed a smile and looked up appreciating Antoinette's honesty. I could not talk about my origins. I didn't have one before Sunshine Shelter.

'That's better. I want to hear you say yes to some things and no to other things. When's your next shift?'

'Tonight.'

'Well, then you don't have time to help anyone today. Get your rest and do what is your priority. I will tell the ladies to stop pestering you.'

'Please don't, Antoinette, I don't want them thinking I'm complaining to you.'

'Now Ruby, this is not high school, and I will tell the ladies what they can and can't do. You nominate one evening only to assist them for no more than two weeks, so just two sessions where they can seek your guidance.'

'That's a good plan. Thank you, Antoinette, I will take

that approach.'

'Good! Off you go to get some rest. Send me an email on which day of the week you want to assist the ladies and I will put up a notice with the day, time, and place when you are available.'

I left Antoinette that morning relieved that she had my back. The nagging thought was why she was going the extra mile for me. Did she suspect I faced the hard knocks of life? Then again, did I?

***

MY SECOND SHIFT was a little better. I served tables, picked up tips and enjoyed the banter from customers. I did not anticipate that my challenges were not over.

It was around 12:30 pm when I left the restaurant. A drizzle fell over town, I stopped under a lamppost, pulled out my black jumper from my bag and drew it across my shoulders. As I strolled with no pressure to hurry, I heard voices behind me and raucous laughter. I sauntered along and that is all I remember.

This crossing is one I feared after reading the daily morning newspapers at Sunshine Shelter.

A man in scrubs stood over me, the bright light above his head made me squint. I tried to sit up and winced as my head fell back against the pillow.

'Who are you? Where am I?'

'Ms you are at the Jacaranda Hospital Emergency Department.'

'Why? Was I ill?'

'You don't recall what happened to you last night?'

'Last night...' I stopped. I drew a blank, unsure of what

happened, and why I was here in the emergency department.

'Think hard, try to recall what happened to you. The police said to call them when you were conscious.'

My heart raced. Had I done something wrong? Did I steal food from the restaurant for Lourdes? I remembered that but had no idea how I ended up in the emergency department. The doctor left to let the police know I was awake. Had I passed out? Why was I struggling to sit up? I was about to face my worst nightmare. The fear of police interrogation. At Sunshine Shelter, we were schooled to feel threatened by the police. Being born with no anchor left us adrift with no defence. No background to ward off the suspicion of guilty by assumption. My records were clean, no drugs, no crimes, just born not knowing why and to whom? Is that my crime?

Every marginalised person has some stigma attached to them based on their economic situation, the absence of access to uptown amenities makes one marginalised. I hated the word, *marginalised*. Who coined it, who said lack of abundant finances was the reason to be deemed marginalised? I made a promise to work on 'unmarginalising' myself. Whatever it took, I was going to earn the respect the 'unmarginalised' were bequeathed!

I waited for the police to arrive. I wish I could sit in a chair and eyeball them across a table.

The good doctor in scrubs returned.

'The police are here to see you. May I bring them in?'

Wow! That was my first sign of gaining respect from someone who did not know me. I nodded as my voice jumped way down my throat.

'Good morning young lady,' the female police officer said, 'how are you feeling?'

Her voice sounded kind; I relaxed a little. Her partner looked at me with no smile, no greeting was forthcoming, and his eyes accused me of everything under a sinful sun!

'Can you tell us what happened last night on your way home?'

'I don't know what happened or why I'm here.'

She explained that I was mugged and she wanted information on who was responsible. How do I explain something I did not see? I looked down at my clothes, they were dusty, and dried blood that might have trickled down the side of my head felt taut.

Who did this to me? Why me?

'An ambulance will be here shortly to take you to the general hospital. You need more checks on your injuries. I will meet you at the hospital to complete my questioning. I need your name and address.'

'Ruby, Ruby Jordan.'

I coughed, shuffled, and whispered, 'I'm in temporary accommodation at the women's shelter in town.'

The male police officer closed his eyes, shook his head and flashed me a burning look, placing a non-verbal guilty charge on my head. Was I ever going to win over the stigma of the homeless, the orphaned, whatever it is I was supposed to be?

'Are you a new tenant there? The policewoman probed.

'Yes, just a few days, it will be a week on Friday.'

'Who can we call to collect you from the hospital after we have finished questioning you?'

'Nobody. I'm new there. Perhaps, Antoinette. She runs the shelter.'

'Is there a family member we could notify?'

I hesitated, knowing that every word I uttered made me more and more a criminal in the male officer's eyes.

I stared at my scuffed shoes, and replied, 'I'm an orphan. I've lived, since birth, in an orphanage. I have no siblings, no relatives.'

As soon as those hollow words were out, I felt a strange release, a sense of freedom in owning who I truly was. There's no shame in that—my developing life experience whispered in my ear. But I was soon to learn it's not so much about being without roots as it is about being a victim as a woman. I was subjected to every test possible, and questioned about why my right-hand index fingernail was broken! I work in a restaurant, in the kitchen, and often as a scullery maid so why would my nails be perfect? They were clean and tidy. Did that not say I was a good, clean-living person?

Antoinette arrived at the hospital, shocked, concerned and confused.

'I'm so sorry you were called out at this hour to verify who I am, Antionette. There is no one else...'

'No need to apologise, how serious are your injuries? Who did this to you?'

'Nothing too serious, I think, although the gash on my head aches a little.'

'A little? I'll speak to the doctor in charge to determine your injuries. The rest the police can sort out.'

I watched Antoinette march up to the doctor on duty.

'You have ten stitches, young lady, so no small gash. The doctor thinks you were struck with a brick. Do you know if your wallet was taken?'

'There was nothing in it. The nurse said I had nothing on me when I arrived at emergency.'

'Robbery must be the motive.'

'I've been checked for physical abuse. I have no recollection of anything other than walking home.'

'That's it, I'm taking you back to the shelter, or home as you kindly call it.'

On the drive back to the shelter Antoinette pulled up two streets away. She looked at me, kindness oozing from her tender eyes. I wondered how she kept up her iron exterior with some of her troublesome guests—a much better word than inmates! Nobody is a prisoner until convicted of some wrongdoing. People like me tend to castigate themselves with an inner critical eye. I breathed deeply and waited for what she was about to ask me.

'Ruby, has any memory returned yet of what happened to you? The gash on your head is evidence of physical violence. You must try to recall what happened, that is the only way the scumbags will be caught and punished.'

'I think that was the only force, the police will have any further information from the hospital I assume. We could call and ask.'

'You have a right to know, I will not be allowed to ask as I'm not your next of kin. At the hospital, you said there was no one else. Only if you are comfortable telling me about your background, I'm all ears. I have a legal obligation to let your next of kin know what has happened to you.'

'I have no next of kin.'

Antoinette's eyes widened. She stared at me for a full two minutes and let out a sigh I could not define. I thought it was not relief, not sadness, but almost a groan, not quite a sigh. I owed her an explanation.

'I'm an orphan, Antoinette.'

'So what? Millions of people are, so who are your adoptive parents, or family?'

I had the urge to bang my head, scream and jump out of the car. I feared what I was about to tell her might alter her perception of me. Now she thought the sun shone out of... I won't go there!

'I was raised in an orphanage, and nobody knows how I got there.'

Her shoulders dropped, and she leaned over and hugged me.

'I'm sorry I pushed you to tell me. I can see this is the hardest thing for you to do, but I don't understand how nobody knows who brought you to the orphanage?'

'That's what I have always been told, so I accepted it.'

'Ruby let's deal with now first, then we can talk about your arrival and life at the orphanage. You are a fine young woman in every sense of the word. How we arrive in this life is not of our doing. Soon we need to put that to bed for you. Let no one take your authenticity from you.'

My eyes stung, and I felt loved and worthy at this moment. An inner voice cautioned that I had to rely on myself. I let Antoinette in and now I feared my secret would taint the aura I created.

Call this my truth-telling crossing. I had to own what would come of it.

***

By MID-MORNING, I summoned the courage to call the female police officer who showed a semblance of kindness when she spoke to me. All she said was there was no other abuse, this was a clear case of robbery and that they would find the offender. I had to work on my memory and had forty-eight hours to come up with some information.

Antoinette was relieved with the information.

'I would have gone door-knocking and taken to the

streets at night to find out who did that to you. You see, I am a child of rape.'

She said that in such a matter-of-fact way, I admired that, but felt a profound sadness that stole my tongue.

'That's another story for another day. You and I have far more in common than you think. Once you have healed, we shall talk. Now you need to call your workplace and tell them you won't be in until the stitches on your head have dissolved. And you are off your duties here this week. Rest and recover.'

'The officer said she would contact my manager. Thankfully I remembered those details. I can still help the ladies with their job applications.'

'No Ruby, you must call your manager and let him know you will be away. Common work ethic ok. The ladies can seek advice this week from the service we provide for job applications. Rest. Gabriella will bring you your meals. I'll check in with her on how you are doing.'

Antoinette slipped back into her manager role, and I had to obey her command to rest.

A MONTH PASSED and I had no further communication from the police department on who my assailant was. I was disappointed and relieved. Seeing my attacker in a police lineup would have been too much to bear. Antoinette stood by me as a maternal protector when the police did not think I deserved justice.

Soon I secured a position at a call centre and started my counselling course at the local college.

My place to rent, a one-bedroom apartment on the west side of town, brought me a sense of accomplishment. I had a place to call *my home*! Privacy, and not answerable to anymore except turning up to my four-evenings-a-week call centre job, and enjoying college by day, felt like I had died and gone to heaven. Well, I could perhaps, with a touch of arrogance, or rather joy, say it was better than that! I had wings to make me soar!

Antoinette came over whenever she could, and I cooked her a meal in gratitude for all she had become in my life.

I was in the sixth month at my rental paradise when Antoinette dropped some news that made my skin crawl.

'Ruby, don't be upset with me. I know you want to be free from the night you were attacked, but I have done some sleuthing. I think, no, I know who was involved in your mugging. Do you want to know who it is? I will respect whatever you want.'

I looked at Antoinette dumbstruck, I had put the incident behind me but had not forgotten it. Labelling it as 'an incident' drew it away from my present existence. My memory might have been blocked by choice. It was my choice. Now I had to decide whether I would allow my dear friend to open that door again. I was vigilant every night when I left the call centre. Fear of that night recurring lurked in my conscious mind.

'Do you think it would help or harm to know? I'm not sure what I want to know right now.'

'Think about it and let me know. I believe it will set you free.'

I paced around my tiny kitchen, went to the bathroom, washed my face, and returned to the kitchen. Antoinette looked at me, long and hard. I knew I could trust her.

'I'm ready to hear it. I need to put this to rest.'

'You sure about this?'

'Yes.' I closed my eyes.

'Lourdes set you up. Her brother was released from

prison that day, and she had him, and a few losers follow you the night you left Vincente's.'

'How do you know this? And why, why would she do this? I was nice to her.'

'Ruby, you are nice to everyone. That's your problem. Her reason is plain old envy that you had a job and she didn't.'

'So, the chances are he can find me again and possibly kill me this time, right?'

'Nope, he's back in prison for some drug deal he was working on.'

'Am I safe then? Please tell me how you know this to be true?'

'After you left the shelter, Lourdes shot her mouth off to someone at breakfast, and Gabriella, always all ears around the ladies, was in a perfect spot, close enough, to record her spilling the beans.'

'Wow! Does Lourdes know that you have access to what she said? I'm not pressing any charges, Antoinette. I want to leave it alone. I don't want things following me for the rest of my life.'

'There's no danger to you now with her brother in jail, and you will be happy to know I called in a friend living interstate to find Lourdes a job. She flew out last week strutting like a peacock. You are safe from that lot. It's up to you whether you want to press charges or not. I have the recorded confession if ever you need it.'

'I'll leave it alone, I think. Thank you, Antoinette! How will I ever repay you?'

'Repay? What do you mean? You treat me like family, and that matters more than anything in my life, especially for someone like me.'

'Someone like you? What do you mean? I have such

respect for what you do. This is the reason I took up the counselling course. I want to give back to struggling individuals. I have a vision for how I will achieve this. Once I have thought it through properly, I will let you in on it. You have inspired me to be a better person.'

'Nonsense! You were a better person the day you arrived at the shelter. I saw that from a mile away. Please don't make me wait too long for this secret plan you have, you hear. I'm getting old and tired every day.'

Antoinette laughed, squeezed my shoulder, washed our coffee mugs and headed for the door.

'Get some sleep, Ruby. You need to be alert for your morning class.'

Sleep eluded me that night. My memory returned before it blacked out. I saw the face of my assailant. A light-haired young man lifted his fist and struck me across the head. That is where I am leaving that drama. I am going places, and I have to keep my undistracted eye on the ball.

***

DAYS ROLLED INTO MONTHS. I enjoyed the call centre work I took on after I left Vincente's. It was here that I built on my people skills and communication side. I grew confident in advising others and making suggestions. Patience is my virtue, I'm not sure where or how I developed that, but I was grateful for it. I tried to offer my trainee counselling skills to the orphanage I once called home. They did not want to hear from me. Once you were out the gate, that was it, you no longer existed. I wondered if this was the case with all who had to leave when they were eighteen. Daniel and Grace did not take my calls and that troubled me. It was my conversation with Antoinette that made me curious.

'Think about it. What is the reason for them turning their backs on you?'

' I don't get it. What are you surmising?'

'You said your background is unknown, that nobody knew how you turned up at your house parents' home, right?' Did it ever cross your mind that such institutions must trace the history or origins of the children they take in?'

'I never thought about it because I was constantly told I arrived in a car seat with no details supplied.'

'And nobody let the police know this happened, that there was an unregistered birth, perhaps?'

'I am curious to know where I came from, but another part of me is petrified. What if the details of my birth are sordid? What if I'm the seed of a criminal or drug addict? I don't know if I could live with that thought.'

'It does not matter. You did not choose to be born to whoever and however, you came to be. There's no shame in that. I think you need to find out. One day when you have children, you will want to tell them about your origins.'

'I am not going to have children. Who will want to have children with me anyway? I don't intend to bring children into this world unless I commit to them.'

'Being an orphan is not a life sentence against the parent you might be! Listen to yourself, Ruby. You have no idea what you are capable of until you allow yourself to do something. You need to get out and about and see life, have some fun, meet a man or woman, and feel the pulse of life. You study and work, and I'm the only person you have let into your life. Why?'

'No time.'

'Really? Or is it that you're afraid to be you, as I know you, with other people.'

'Please, let's talk about something else.'

Antoinette's cocked head and frown made me nervous to admit she might be right.

'Do you want to know anything about your history?'

'I think I do... but where do we start?'

'Research, my dear Ruby. Beginning with the births recorded in the year you were born. Then we investigate the orphanage and get inside the lives of the people who work there.'

I sighed, 'How are we going to do all of that? I am keen to finish my counselling qualification.'

'That will go on. I have contacts, legal contacts that we can approach.'

'That will cost a fortune! I don't have that kind of money with my meagre call centre earnings.'

'Did you hear what I said, 'contacts,' for whom I have done favours before? Now it's time to call in a favour or two from them. What do you say, Ruby girl?'

Now I fixed my steady gaze on Antoinette. This pint-sized powerhouse of determination.

I nodded, 'Yes, I am ready to know the truth.'

Antoinette stood up, twirled around, and laughed, 'That's my girl!'

You know what they say, once you open a door, you must face whatever music comes your way. With Antoinette, I felt safe that I could handle anything. Some things perhaps....

***

Antoinette was true to her word. I studied, she investigated and the year I graduated with my counselling qualification, she had found a piece of the puzzle to my shadowed life.

She arranged a coffee meeting with a woman who said she had a child at the same hospital I was born in. How could I trust this when there was no record of where I was born? I trusted Antoinette and went along with her arrangement to meet the stranger who might know something about me. At the eleventh hour, I chickened out. Petrified. What if my birth was horrific? Antoinette met the lady who agreed to be recorded. This is what I heard:

A baby named Ruby was born at a downtown hospital to a young unmarried woman. The hospital chaplain and nun spent long sessions talking to the young mother about why giving her baby up for adoption was better. The young woman wept at night. The lady told Antoinette her bed was to the left of the young mother. On the third morning, when the chaplain arrived, the young woman's bed was empty, and the nursery staff reported her baby as missing. I halted the revelation, fearful to hear more yet wanting to know. The woman said a man called asking what had happened to the young woman. He spoke to the lady in the next bed.

' Who is this man? Does he have a name?'

'Shush, Ruby, just listen carefully.' Antoinette urged.

The soft voice on the recording said when she asked the man for his name—he said he was Dan. Dan who? I wanted to know more about his relationship with the young woman who disappeared from the hospital.

The voice in the recording said Dan told her he was the baby's father.

I looked at Antoinette in disbelief as my fear mounted. My head asked what my heart always felt.

Was Daniel my father? Not just my house father, but my connection by blood and birth father?

'Is it Daniel?' I asked Antoinette through a fog of tears. The recording ended there.

The woman did not want to be recorded saying that Dan was married and that the young woman left baby Ruby at the front door of Daniel's and Grace's cottage at Sunshine Shelter. She left a note on the baby.

This is Ruby. Love her like your own.

No papers on the child's birth were included in the worn-out car seat she was found in.

Was this to be my final crossing? My coming to terms with why dear sweet Daniel, Danny-Dad, never told me I was his child. Was it enough for him to have me under his roof, watch over me, and place rules on whether I could spend a weekend with Greta? Questions went off in my head like a fireworks display. Did Grace know I was Daniel's daughter?

I chose my final crossing. I wanted nothing from Daniel. My identity and family history would remain elusive. Common sense told me he would deny that he was my father, perhaps to avoid the shame of having me believe I was lucky I arrived at his and Grace's door.

I have a dream for a big future, and I have Antoinette.

I had everything I would ever need.

CONFIDENCE QUEST

Changing the course of one's life does not resolve the past, it redefines the present until the lesson is acknowledged. In one lifetime many lessons arrive to sculpt the intended design.

CONFIDENCE QUEST

There are some who say, 'not another story on bullying' and there are those who will say, 'great to have new voices on an endless social issue.' What about you dear reader?

I AM the middle child to my parents and accept I was supported by my older sibling and overshadowed by my younger sibling. That was not an issue for me. My parents were fair and loving. 'So, what's the problem, girl' I hear you say.

I looked different to my siblings, the only one with dark skin and green eyes. Dad's eyes and mum's dark skin tone. Some people told me I had striking looks, whatever that was supposed to mean, but I liked hearing that. My brain could absorb many things which made me a good student. I was at a selective school for what they called the 'gifted.' It was enough that I was a gift to my parents, I did not need to be a gift anywhere else. And I wasn't.

My looks were the subject of lots of schoolyard chatter.

The conversations would stop when I walked by. You have that instinctive empath energy when someone is talking about you. It was only when the notes arrived inside my schoolbooks and then pasted onto my locker door that I knew I had to tell my mother about the harassment.

Freak of nature. Feline face. Evil witch. Mixed up.

It hurt deep to my core when these comments turned up. A soul-shattering hurt. Who was a friend and who was a foe?' The school failed to identify the perpetrator or perhaps there was more than one. My mother appealed to the headmaster to install surveillance cameras near the lockers. All she got was, 'Sorry, no funding for that. 'I was offered counselling for my torment. In an inverted world, the criminals are set free, and victims get a counselling reward. I am all for counselling but putting a permanent end to the torment is favourable. It got worse in senior high school. My mother moved me to a culturally diverse school. No selective, gifted or any such label, school. The school was a vibrant hive of acceptance where individuals were just that. Free to be whoever they were. I loved it! My last two years of high school birthed my confidence. I had dance lessons, played the piano, and sang in the school choir. My looks melted into the universal acceptance motto of the school, 'One under the sky of humanity.' Lime Tree High School made me feel welcome and significant to the life of the school. I made a graduation speech in my final year of high school. These lines brought my year group to their feet, clapping for what seemed like forever. My words struck a chord with them.

We have had our highs and lows through our schooling years but never forget no matter where you come from, who your family is, or the hue of your skin – the power to be uniquely you, rests with YOU.

MY FIRST YEAR at university came with its own set of stress factors. I'm not talking about the academic side of things. Oh no. It was as if I was starting life for the first time. The question, 'where are you from?' and the condescending, 'it's lovely to have people of colour among us.' You read that right. 'People of colour', and 'among us.' That blew my confidence. My voice retreated to a place where I did not want to be heard or seen. Halfway through the first year of my law degree, I left to join the army. I figured I had to be tough in every way to gain respect and recognition. My parents were devastated but respected my choice.

I knew my physical limitations but had to overcome them quickly if I hoped to gain my stripes of acceptance.

As the weeks turned into months at the Sigma Barracks in Camp Alpha, my friendly soft side imbibed from my father clashed with my peers. At the Sigma Barracks, no one spoke to me. My male peers sought me out for conversations. First, they were generally from the coffee I preferred to the type of music I liked. Then I sensed the intensity of dominance. One officer always came in a bit too close to speak to me. At first, I secretly named him Foul Breath but changed when I sensed an awkwardness within him. He told me the officers in his barracks referred to me as SE. He did not know what it represented, and I naively thought it was a rank denotation for a rookie soldier. I never asked what SE represented and stupidly responded when called. Foul Breath was Nick. He was nice to me, and I absorbed his acceptance like a dry sponge. We spoke about my family, and he seemed genuinely interested in my life outside the camp. An odd friendship developed. That is how I perceived it. We had coffee together, he taught me how to cope with the physical demands of the army. I was overjoyed to have a mentor. Little did I know that was alienating me from my female peers at the Sigma Barracks. I had no one to talk to about my level of discomfort when things changed with Nick. The red flags were flying high, but I blocked them. He asked for exclusivity in our friendship which he preferred to call a partnership.

The subtle manipulation had begun. Now I know I was being seduced, groomed for his entertainment. Each time I took a day pass, he would ask if he could join me, or if I would cancel the time away. My monthly weekend visits to my parents dwindled. My mother made her displeasure known in her messages.

> Rosa, when are you coming home? We miss you.

It took a few months before I told her about Nick. Her reaction scared me.

> Who is this man that you have cast off your family for? If you like, you can bring him to visit us one weekend.

I had visions of my older brother interrogating Nick, and my younger brother committing every word and action to memory to role-play later in a fit of hysterical laughter.

We laughed a lot as kids. Everything turned into something laughable.

Nick was just a friend, and I was uncomfortable about having him around my family. I never told him about the invitation from my mother and stayed at the camp on my weekends off.

Nick suggested we go away together because he wanted to teach me how to fish. I agreed even though I had no interest in fishing. I never knew how to say no to anyone. I had never been away with a friend before, and I was his only army buddy—his only friend. How could I refuse?

We drove to Lake Mercy which was a three-hour drive from the army base. He booked a small cabin recessed in the woods with a snaking footpath to the lake. His mood lifted when we arrived. He went out of his way to please me.

'What would you like for dinner? I have seafood, chicken, and beef to cook any way you want.'

'No, Nick, this is your weekend getaway. You rarely leave the base so enjoy this time. I can see to myself.'

The sudden change in his tone, 'I won't accept your refusal,' scared me.

It was high-pitched and slow. Then his demeanour morphed before my eyes. His lips stretched in mocked pain as he reprimanded himself, 'Stop that, Nick, Rosie is good.' This was the first time he referred to me as Rosie. Nobody did, I was always Rosa to all who knew me. Fear took hold, and I quickly made light of the moment.

'Rosa,' I laughed, 'you said, 'Rosie.'

'Rosie, Rosie, Rosie.' The same strange tone.

I decided to leave it there.

'When will we go down to the water to fish?'

'Not today. Mama said, we must eat first, or we might drown.'

His behaviour baffled me. He spoke like one possessed by a frightened child who was afraid to be punished if he did not eat before he went to the lake.

He proceeded to light the barbecue and grilled the seafood he had already spiced. The small fridge in the cabin was stocked. I don't know when he did that. I imagined the cabin was part of a serviced resort.

It was isolated.

Nick was subdued during dinner. We sat outdoors under a makeshift canopy with the blankets he pulled out of his backpack. He jumped up with excitement, clapping his hands, and asking if I would like a glass of wine.

'How did you manage to get us wine?'

'No questions, Rosie.'

'Thank you, Nick.'

Around midnight we parted company. I needed a good night's sleep to be ready to learn how to fish the next day.

Sleepless hours later, I heard a car pull up outside the cabin and indiscernible voices muttered and the vehicle drove off. It must have been 3 am when I fell asleep. At 7 am I woke with a jolt to the aroma of brewing coffee. There was no sign of Nick. I showered and poured myself a cup of coffee and waited for Nick to arrive.

I am ashamed to admit I searched through Nick's bedroom cupboards. There was nothing specific I was looking for other than some insight into the odd behaviour he presented last night. At the bottom of his cupboard, I found an old family photo album. A photograph of a boy sitting on a bench with an old man and woman suggested that Nick might have been an only child. The boy was in all the photographs in the album. He never smiled in any of them. His posture was stiff and upright, his eyes hollow and sad. I placed the album back where I found it and searched through the kitchen cupboards. The dishes were old, discoloured as though they had lived in the cupboards for a century. Nick said he booked a cabin in the woods near the lake for the weekend, but an inner voice suggested he had been here before.

At noon Nick returned, reeking of alcohol. After his odd behaviour last night, I dared not question him about where he was. Anyway, I had no hold over him and he had nothing over me.

'Rosie, get ready we're going fishing.'

His unsteady gait bothered me. How on earth would he teach me how to hold a fishing rod when he could barely keep still? I reminded myself that I was alone with him, and he could get aggressive if I refused.

I offered to drive the car down to the water, but he insisted we walk.

It was quiet at the lake. Nick made several attempts to get the rod hooked and baited without success. I summoned all the patience I could and sat on the grassy knoll beside him. When he reached to touch my thigh, I instinctively pushed his hand away.

'Come on Rosie, don't be like that.'

'We are friends, Nick, nothing else, ok?'

'Why did you come here with me, sexy eyes?'

The penny dropped. The officers in his barracks called me SE and he knew what it meant. Here I was again labelled on my looks. Sexy Eyes was a new tag added to the ones I had accrued over the years. I was uncomfortable and knew I had to find a way to leave this god-forsaken place to be safe.

Two hours later we headed back to the cabin.

'We are having a party tonight. Four officers and their girls are coming over.'

'Oh, I didn't know you had invited them over.'

'I didn't, they invited themselves when they knew I was coming to the cabin with you.'

It was obvious that Nick was bullied in his barracks. He bent to the demands of his fellow officers to feel valued. In some ways, we were more alike than we were different.

'What can I help to prepare for tonight's party?'

'Nothing. The guys are bringing the party snacks and music. We can relax.'

I was here with Nick and not included in any of his weekend plans, other than the non-event fishing expectation. He appeared to inhabit a bubble and occasionally acknowledged my presence.

'I need a nap, I've been up all night.'

He did not explain why he hadn't slept. I recalled hearing hushed voices and a vehicle driving away. I asked no questions to avoid setting him off. You think you know a person until you are alone with them in an isolated place. I allowed myself to be persuaded to join Nick on this short getaway. He wanted to do this for me. Every experience is expected to educate and transform the individual. Not for me, I was stuck in a rut, the rut of my past. I could leave while Nick slept. It was returning to the army base after having deserted him that scared me. My commander was a force to be feared. I planned to leave after Nick's party tonight. If I humiliated him by leaving before that, my life would be far worse than it already was at the base.

This decision is one I regretted.

***

Four officers arrived at the cabin around 8 pm minus their partners. I looked forward to some female company, but a boys' night it was set to be. An easygoing first two hours with lots of drinks and laughter was bearable until one officer turned to me.

'Bored SE? You don't seem to be having fun. Don't like our company?' His sardonic tone and narrowed eyes irritated me.

'Not at all, I did look forward to meeting your partners, though.'

He tossed his head back and laughed and stopped abruptly.

'Female company is what she craves. Hear that, Nick?'

Nick said nothing. His gaze fixated on the floor. The tips of his ears were blood red. His lowered head was much like the little boy in the family photo album.

My heart skipped a beat when a gun cocked behind me. The officer, much younger than the others, grabbed my hair and placed his gun on the back of my neck. My body twitched from head to toe.

'Is this what excites you, SE?'

I whispered, 'Stop this now before there is an accident we cannot undo!'

Horrible drunken guttural grunting and snorting sounds filled the small cabin.

A chair scraped against the floor as Nick dashed out of the cabin like a hunted rabbit. Nobody went after him. He abandoned me in my hour of dire need.

My hair was pulled to lift me off the seat. I was thrown to the floor, and as the young officer reached down to grab my hair again, I kicked him in the groin, I heard laughter and jeers from his peers.

'Ewwww... ouch... SE got you where it hurts most! Ouch!'

While the jeering went on, I did a runner for the door that Nick had left wide open in his haste to escape.

The night air brushed against my skin and a cool trickling down my nose tasted like blood on my lips. I ran for my life. My head ached but my legs kept striding. My training gave me the stamina to keep running. I had no sense of direction in this wilderness. I let my internal GPS guide me. In the blackness of the woods, I tripped on a log and heard the crunching of dry fallen leaves as the men hunted me.

I did not want to be another statistic on violence against women. My mother imprinted that rape was something no one got over. These thoughts claimed all my headspace as I kept running into the unknown. How did my mother know this? That question would remain unanswered if I did not get out of the woods tonight. I grazed myself against dry, splintered tree branches—dried in the heat of the season. Blood left a trail for my pursuers.

I ducked down when I saw a flash of light, thinking it might be a torchlight. The beam of light grew closer. I heard a rumbling vehicle engine. I was close to a road. I followed the vehicle sounds and ended up on a narrow stretch of road. A truck was ahead of me. I flung my arms into the air, hoping I would be noticed. The truck stopped and reversed to where I was. The driver saw me!

A gun crawled out of an open back window.

I dived back into the long dry grass and kept running.

I had to survive. That was my only thought.

I was unprotected in this unfamiliar territory. I joined the army to boost my confidence, and here I was exposed to human cruelty and the harsh elements of nature. Studying law and building a career in it could have given me the confidence I craved. My family had no idea where I was or that Nick was not my romantic other.

In my quest for confidence, had I messed up my life?

The choices we make lead us to people and places. There is a grand design beyond our choices that puts us through the rigour of life for a clear sense of self-definition. These thoughts calmed my fear as I continued to run through the woods.

The laughter grew closer behind me. The men were gaining ground on me. It was a full moon night and everything that moved in an upright position was discernible. I alternated between running and crawling on my hands and knees.

By some lucky stroke, I reached the lake. The silvery glow on the water's surface was welcoming and daunting. I was an intrepid swimmer, winning gold medals in all the competitions my mother chose for me. For her being a strong swimmer was an important survival skill. She emphasised that but never told me or my siblings why she believed this. I questioned my lack of confidence as perhaps being caused by the many answers I needed but never received. Was it fair to blame my mother for this? My cousins bullied me too, playing with my quiet, shy nature. My mother turned the other way when I was bullied by my family. Her middle sister would often say, 'Stop molly-coddling her, Ariana, let her toughen up. You don't want *your life* recurring in Rosa. Tough love finally got you through. You should thank me for that.' The conversation I overheard between my mother and her sister made no sense. My mother was strong, needing no one to pave her way. She stood up for her values and earned great respect as a formidable mother and police-woman. My thoughts wandered around, clinging to my sanity. I feared if I plunged into the lake, I would have no idea where I was heading. When your life is threatened you take risks. That was my lesson on confidence building. Risk-taking.

I glided into the water, boots, jacket, jeans, and all, not wanting to make a big splash that would alert the men to where I was. The water was calming. I waded further in until I heard thundering boots in the woods behind me. A quick dive below the surface of the water offered me brief protection. I could hear angry voices, but words were unclear from where I was. To my utter relief, the voices and trudging boots faded. I floated to the surface and swam at an even pace. The moon, now shadowed in half a cloud, secluded me from visibility. I had no idea of the time. I had to keep going. Music was my inspiration in times of stress. I hummed a lullaby I heard our neighbour, Arlo, sing to his little boy. I must have swum for at least an hour when I saw a cluster of lights to the right of where I was. Although my muscles ached, I picked up my pace to reach land.

I arrived on a cobbled surface and struggled to pull myself up onto my feet. It was raining, the air was cold. I sat on the cobbled water's edge, rubbing my legs to warm them and slowly got onto my feet. A road to the left of the lake, above the embankment, seemed to lead to a village. I walked towards the cluster of lights until I arrived at a run-down petrol station. It was shut but had a buzzer with a sign that read:

Ring if in desperate need only, please.

I was in desperate need to know where I was and had to call the police. Hesitation and cautiousness would not serve me now. I pressed the buzzer and waited. Ten minutes later

I was still waiting and pressed the buzzer again. Someone shuffled inside the petrol shop front.

'Hold your horses, I'm coming!'

The steps were heavy and the voice deep.

The door flung open. A rotund woman with a mop of curly hair peered at me.

'We're closed. What is it that you want?'

'I'm so sorry to disturb you at this hour, but I'm in a desperate situation. I'd like to use a phone, if possible, please. A group of men are threatening my life,' I stammered, only because my teeth chattered from the cold.

'Group of men? I see none.' She peered out into the darkness. 'Did your car get stuck in the rain? Looks like you've been walking a long way, you're drenched to the skin.'

'No, er... no, I swam across the lake.'

The woman's eyes grew ten times larger than they were five seconds ago. Suddenly she bellowed, 'Harry, get down here!'

'Who's Harry, ma'am? I assure you I'm no criminal. I'm from the army.'

'Harry, hurry, we have trouble at the door! Get down here now!'

'I'll leave, I don't want to cause any problems. I need to inform my army base about my whereabouts, but I don't know where I am.'

'Get inside,' she whispered, pulling my arm. 'You need to dry off first then make your calls. Come this way, I'll show you to the bathroom. Fresh towels are in the drawer next to the wash bowl.'

Harry appeared in his flannel pyjamas outside the bathroom door.

His thinning white hair was a contrast to the woman's

cascading curls. I felt awful for having disturbed this elderly couple. Brave couple.

'What have we got here, Maeve?'

'Not sure, Harry, she could even be a runaway soldier.'

They spoke as though I was invisible compounding my lack of self-worth.

'I'm not a runaway nor am I a criminal. You'll soon know when the police get here. What area is this?'

'You really don't know where you are. Did you hit your head along the way?'

I thought Maeve was mocking me but realised she was serious when she shook her head and peered into my eyes.

'I'm not concussed. These parts are unfamiliar to me because I'm an out-of-towner.'

'A stranger is what you mean,' Harry said with a suspicious look in his eye.

I nodded.

'Get dry, I'll make you a mug of cocoa and you can make your telephone calls.'

'Thank you.' I dared not say I had never had a mug of cocoa in my life.

Maeve asked me to explain my situation to them before I made any calls.

'I should tell you, my dear, the police around here will not be very helpful. For one, it is a small station and secondly, they work on wooden wheels, so don't expect anybody to come out here now unless you are dead!'

After an hour of surmising what was the best thing to do, Harry suggested calling my family before I called the commander at the army base. There was no way I could call my mother without getting an earful at this hour of the morning. I looked at the clock in the hallway to the rear of the petrol station. It was 3:35 am. Maeve recommended calling her nephew who was a retired police officer for advice.

'I appreciate your help but feel awful about disturbing your nephew at this unearthly hour.'

'Sleep on the couch until the sun rises, and we'll call him then. How does that suit you?'

I thanked Maeve and Harry and accepted their couch for a few hours of shut-eye. Once alone with my thoughts, I wondered if the cabin was closer than I thought. Could my swimming across the lake have been in vain? My fears were aplenty. A doubting mind, the bane of my existence, demolished my confidence.

Getting lost was in my DNA. A childhood experience scarred me. I wandered off during a family outing at the fair travelling through our hometown. I remember my hand being snatched by a man who asked me where my parents were and, at that moment, I knew I was lost. When the man lifted me into his arms, I kicked and screamed. I was three years old. He plonked me off at the fair announcement table and left. A woman asked me my name and my parents' names. She announced that she had a lost child named Rosa waiting to be claimed at the announcement table. It seemed like forever until my mother walked up to collect me. Much later in life when the incident was recalled during family gatherings, I was made a laughingstock for wandering off not too far from my mother. I hated those conversations that put a negative spotlight on me.

Maeve was the first to rise and found me wide-eyed on the couch.

'Oh dear, looks like you have not slept a wink. I'll bring coffee over soon. I must bring in the newspaper delivery for the store.'

'Let me help you do that.'

'That's lovely, thank you. It's a chilly morning, pull the little blanket across your shoulders.'

Maeve offered maternal comfort to a stranger. She trusted me on instinct alone. I felt secure in this space with her.

We brought in the newspapers as a vehicle pulled up.

'Go to the back dear, stay there. Harry will be out soon to start his day serving customers.'

I lingered in the passage behind the storefront.

'Good morning, I'm from the army base and last night a trainee soldier disappeared. Has a young woman been around here, shopping for food and other essentials?'

I could barely breathe waiting for Maeve's response.

'We've just opened, sir, not a soul passed here until you arrived now. Sorry, what did you say your name was? I'm a bit hard of hearing.' Maeve laughed.

'Nick Miles, please call me on this number if you suspect the woman is in the area. '

I pressed myself against the passage wall, faint from knowing that Nick was a few steps away. He sounded officious, unlike the crazed man I experienced when I was alone with him.

'Give me a description or show me a photo of this person please to be sure I'm not calling you after every young woman stops by.'

'Sure, I have a photo on my phone.'

'Thanks, oh she's a pretty young thing. I'll be sure to let you know if she stops here.'

I heard the cash register draw shut.

'Have a good day,' Maeve said and received no reply.

A startled Harry stared at me pressed against the passage wall. I put my fingers to my lips and waited until Maeve peered around the corner.

'That was close! I was sweating under my jumper. You obviously heard that conversation. Who is he?'

'He is the one who ran off and left me. We were at the cabin together.'

'Is he your boyfriend?' Maeve frowned, leaving me concerned that she might be dubious about my story.

'I thought he was a friend until we got to the cabin, and the other four men arrived.'

'You are lucky you made it here alive. I'm having doubts about calling the police. It's better to let your family know. Harry and I took you in and we don't even know your name.'

'I'm Rosa Armand from the Sigma Barracks at Camp Alpha. I am grateful for what you and Harry have done to protect me.'

'Right, let's get that coffee and I'll call my nephew, David, over to help you get to someplace safe, and advise you on how to proceed. It's not safe here with anybody and everybody coming through the store doors.'

***

DAVID ARRIVED AT 9 AM. Maeve ensured I had a hearty sausage and egg breakfast, despite my protests.

'Rosa Armand, I believe, stationed at Sigma, Camp Alpha. I took the liberty of googling you after Maeve called me regarding your situation. You are highly credited by your Chief Commander.'

'Thank you for seeing me, David.'

'How did you get yourself into this mess?'

The mess was not what I created. My confidence in sharing the intimate details of my situation took a knock with his comment. I let it pass as I explained how I came to be at the cabin with Nick, and the arrival of the officers without their partners.

'Too much niceness in my book is a terrible thing. But you know that, already.'

I was being lectured to in my mother's style and had to accept all that came at me if I hoped to have David's generous offer of assistance for my safety.

'The best way forward is to get you to a safe place and then report this to your commander and family. The five men must have returned to Camp Alpha or are on their way there. It will be interesting to see if they report you as a missing person.'

'Thank you, David, I agree getting to a safe place is a priority. I could get a hotel out of town and lie low there and inform my commander.'

'That will be inviting the return of last night's situation. Let me be the face for you and do the reporting after I place you in safety. Everything I do will be in consultation with how you feel about my choices.'

I sighed, close to tears that David was collaborative. Not the bullying retired police officer I initially thought he was.

'An ex-police partner of mine lives on a farm up north, she will gladly offer you accommodation and prime protection until it's safe for you to return to Camp Alpha or wherever you choose to go. How's that?'

'That's great thank you. I hate being an imposition. I'm ever so grateful I ended up at Maeve's door.'

'You are lucky you did. Maeve is one great lady. I owe her a lot. Now, are you sure you can put up with the likes of me on an eight-hour drive up north? Let me make that call to Prue first.'

'No complaints from me. You're saving my life.'

Maeve packed chicken pieces, pastries, a few rounds of ham and cheese sandwiches in an esky, and two large flasks of coffee ready to go by 11:30 am.

'Rosa cannot step out of the vehicle so this should tide you over. I've called to let June and Avril know that you will make a bathroom stop on your journey. No public toilet visits. It's risky with camera sightings that the army can dig up before you reach the north. Here are some hats and jackets to travel incognito.'

'Oh, Maeve. Thank you! How will I ever repay you and Harry, now David.'

'By staying alive, dear, to give back to communities in need.'

My eyes welled up, I nodded and reached to hug her.

'Stay safe, Rosa, listen to David in all be advises. David's van is in the garage so get in and lie low until you are out on the open road.'

This welcoming trio seemed seasoned in how they orchestrated my exit.

At 11:45 am David and I eased out of Glistening Waters. I caught a glimpse of the signpost at the end of the cross-road, a short distance from the petrol station.

The first hour on the drive north was quiet after David asked if I was comfortably lying at the rear of the van. I would have to stretch my legs every couple of hours but did not dare to let him know.

'What music do you like, Rosa? I have just about anything in this van. That's if you like to listen to music on a road trip. David obviously travelled a lot and music was his companion, yet he selflessly allowed me quiet time for the first hour. Who were these angel workers? Then my cautioning mind kicked in, what if I was being abducted? Time will tell.

'I love jazz, contemporary jazz or any era, but whatever you choose is fine by me. Music will make the journey seem brief.'

He turned on the sounds of Herbie Hancock.

Another hour passed when he announced that June's bathroom stop would be coming up in half an hour. My legs needed stretching more than my bladder did.

'Tell me a bit about June, so I know how to respond when we meet.'

'You won't meet June. She will leave the key to her outside bathroom for us, we use it, lock it up and leave the key where we found it. It's a secluded area so we can stretch our legs. I estimate we will get to Prue around nine-thirty-ish.'

This was a tight operation. David seemed to be part of a sophisticated vigilante organisation that saved damsels in distress. Everything worked like clockwork and cruised into what he had to do with Maeve's support. Harry played a neutral role, not saying much.

June's property was a small holding. The dirt track to the main building was ten minutes from the freeway exit. David pulled up outside a thatched structure and returned with the key. He drove for another five minutes until we arrived at a whitewashed building that looked like horse stables. The bathroom was at the back. Neat and well stocked with all the amenities from a shower loaded with products one would find in a hotel bathroom. A small room to the left of the bathroom had a kettle, microwave, and small fridge. David told me to meet him in the kitchenette.

'Wow! June is well set up here. Please thank her for this when you can.'

David smiled and tucked into the lunch Maeve packed. We walked around the building a few times, left the keys where David found them and drove into the afternoon sun. It was a clear day; we drove past rolling fields that looked like they had not seen rain in ages. After our halfway stop, David seemed ready to drop his guard.

'You haven't asked me anything about myself. If you want a fast five minutes, I'm open to any questions you might have?'

I took a deep breath knowing I had to select my questions wisely if I wanted depth in the answers or information David provided.

'Thank you for that. I'll start by asking if Maeve raised you.'

'Smart question! She sure did. My mother was Maeve's sister. She died when I was six months old having suffered physical trauma from my abusive, violent father. All that I am is thanks to Maeve.'

'Oh, I'm so sorry David, your poor mother.'

'Life happens in ways we never envision. Right, next question?'

'When did you retire from the police force, and why before the retirement age?'

'Ah, two in one question. I must look young to you,' he laughed, 'to be asked such a question. I served twenty years in the force. I loved my work.'

He was silent on the second part of my question.

'Why did you leave?'

He clenched his jaw and blinked a hundred times per second.

'My daughter, just sixteen years old, died in a home invasion intended to put me out. She jumped between me and the intruder when he pointed the gun at me. He targeted me because his little brother was behind bars for being the mule for a drug cartel. I was the chief investigating officer on that case.'

'I seem to be asking questions that hit a sensitive nerve, I'm so sorry.'

'Don't be sorry. It tells me you have great army skills. I think this tells you why I dedicate my life to helping women facing trauma of every sort.'

'Oh David, I don't think I should ask any more questions. I know all that I need to know.'

'Sure?'

'Yeah, thank you. Do you have any questions for me?'

'Perhaps, I will ask a few before we arrive at Avril's rest stop.'

'Shoot, I'm listening.'

'It will be dark in half an hour so you can sit up rather than lie down.'

'Great, I'm afraid I'll have a sore back when we arrive at the safe house.'

'Prue will help you out with that. My first question is why won't you let your family know that you are on the run from danger?'

'That question involves a long and complex answer. If you're ready, I could be answering that all the way to Prue's place.'

David nodded and gave me a thumbs-up.

I explained it all from being a middle child to facing bullying more of the verbal and emotional type rather than physical abuse. The failed completion of my law degree was not something I ever wished to share with others. It felt easy telling David that I dropped my law studies to join the army. I emphasised my non-romantic friendship with Nick. The bit I left out was my eroded self-concept and level of confidence. I did not want to encourage passive aggressiveness between David and I. He was a great listener and never once stopped me to ask for clarification.

'Wow, Rosa, you've been fighting a lone battle. You are going to find Prue a great ally, I assure you. Wait until you hear her story to feel gratified that what you are facing is not half as bad.'

How did I get myself into a situation where I was pouring out my heart to a stranger? I valued privacy like nothing else. What I told David could not be removed. I feared he would judge me for being a weak soldier.

We arrived at Avril's property. A modern townhouse with nobody at home. David picked up a key from under the floorboard on the front porch and we entered a cosy home.

'Avril's away on contract work but allows me access to her place whenever I'm travelling. She asks no questions. Just as I like it.'

The home was small but exuded a charm and warmth I'd never experienced before. It was a home that celebrated family. The lounge walls and the top of the piano displayed family group photographs. A family of four, a mother, and three children, and larger groups smiled in beautifully framed photographs. A familiar face in the group photograph stared back at me. I studied it and gradually realised it was a younger Maeve. David was outside smoking. We took a forty-five-minute stop at Avril's home. I felt guilty for studying the photographs in a stranger's home—a hospitable stranger's home.

David popped his head in saying it was time to leave if we hoped to get to Prue's place at a reasonable hour. A house telephone rang in three quick rounds and stopped.

'We should hurry, Rosa, that ringing telephone is

persistent and before someone comes over, we need to get out of here.'

David turned off the lights he had turned on, left the passage light burning as he found it, placed the key back under the floorboard and we sped back to the freeway.

'Gosh, that felt unnerving for a second! Do you think someone might have come over while we were there?'

'It's never happened before, so that rattled me a bit.'

'It's lovely of Avril to share her home with people like me. She must trust you and Maeve.'

'Yeah, she's been great supporting what we do.'

The itch to ask if young Maeve was indeed in the photograph in the house grew.

'David, I hope you don't think it sneaky of me but I looked at the photographs in Avril's lounge room. I thought I saw Maeve in the group photograph. Would that be right?'

I heard David sigh, then pause before he looked at me.

'You are observant, not sneaky, you have a keen eye. The person is Maeve. Avril is my ex; we lost our daughter in the shooting I mentioned. Our marriage crumbled after Lucy's death. I have not seen Avril since Lucy's funeral. She communicated through Maeve and joined us in supporting abused women in their safe removal and relocation.'

It was my turn to sigh and be silent. David was a complex man but a man with a heart of gold. There was nothing I could say except extend my gratitude for what he and his team were doing to help me. The rest of the journey to Prue's farm was subdued.

***

A LAMPPOST LIT the entrance signpost.

Prudence Estate - Enter at Your Own Risk.

David got out of the van and opened the gate, drove, and stopped again to shut the gate. I heard dogs barking in the distance. The headlights made a pack of four agile Dobermans visible. They were snarling and barking. I froze in my seat.

'David, I'm not getting off the van. These dogs are killers.'

'Only if threatened and when Prue gives the command.'

'Have they killed before?'

'You'll have to ask Prue. I just know they protect Prue and her property.'

'What about her guests.'

'Them too unless she needs to give the command to attack.'

'Oh, dear! I am going to be uneasy around here.'

'You might feel differently after you've met Prue.'

I shut my eyes with a prayer on my lips as the dogs continued growling and jumping up against the van as we drove down to the farmhouse. When we crossed a speed hump, the house floodlights turned the garden into a sports field. Everything else was in darkness. David pulled up in a demarcated parking bay. Someone in a trench coat dashed out from the majestic house and led the dogs away.

'Who was that?'

'Property manager, I think.'

A large wooden door flung open. A long-haired, lean woman appeared. Her arched eyebrows and pale powdered face gave her a surreal gothic look. She smiled and extended her hands to welcome us.

'Ah David,' then she looked at me, 'Welcome to your new home, Rosa, for however long you shall stay.'

Prue's regal manner created the urge to curtsy. Her voice was deep, like that of a smoker.

'Thank you,' I whispered.

'You both must be exhausted. I have your usual room ready, David. You should stay the night, but you must leave at the crack of dawn. Rosa, follow me to your room, then we shall meet in the sitting room to get a little acquainted.'

The room Prue allocated to me was gigantic. It had a four-poster bed and a large painting of her four Dobermans above the bed. I stiffened at the thought of many sleepless nights that would follow.

'Thank you, Prue, May I call you, Prue?'

'Prue, 'P' whatever you like,' her hoarse laughter echoed into the hallway behind her.

'I'll shower and meet you and David in the sitting room soon.'

Prue shut the door behind her.

The house felt like an ancient palace. High ornate ceilings and pillars defied what I knew of farmhouses. I felt excitement surge at the possibility of roaming outdoors and investigating the indoors. Prue appeared to be an interesting character. David chose this as the last outpost before justice would be served and my safety ensured. I hoped so.

A beautiful kaftan was laid out on the bed. A pair of sequinned black slippers sat on the floor next to the bed. From a fugitive on the run, I felt like a princess in a fairy tale. I was nervous about my first up-close meeting with Prue. David was around, and that comforted me.

Prue sat in a large, regal chair, draped in tiger skin. From behind she appeared to be a young woman. The lines on her lived face and greying hair were the only markers of her seniority. Living in this palatial home would require tremendous energy to get from place to place. I wondered if tomorrow would present a different view of this majestic-by-night house.

'Oh, there you are, Rosa. David has retired for the night. I'm afraid you're stuck with me. Tea? Coffee or a glass of wine?'

'Tea, please. Will I see David before he leaves?'

'No, his part ends here. I run the ship to your safe return wherever you choose as that place. David will call your commander when I give him the thumbs up.'

David had quickly become my anchor. His honesty won me over. Prue was pragmatic. That scared me. I craved comfort as a lost soul, I suppose. It's an odd situation I find myself in. I chose the army to harden my soft side, my vulnerabilities, and my need to feel secure. I was not there yet and wonder if I would ever get there. I was lost in my thoughts when I suddenly became aware that Prue was talking to me.

'Rosa, Rosa... you must be exhausted. We can chat tomorrow. I wanted a heads up on what outcome you desire from your situation.'

'Oh, sorry Prue, my mind wanders off sometimes on that very subject. I'm not sure, to be honest. Safety first, I think.'

'Will you go back to your base once the men are held to account for what they have done?'

'I would like to, but technically they have not physically harmed me, and I don't think there will be consequences for them.'

'Really? You would go back? Guaranteed there will be no consequences for those monsters. Who knows what else they have done to terrify other women.'

'As I said, I am processing what I should do. Your questions are helping me to think clearly, thank you.'

'Have your tea and go to bed. We'll convene tomorrow. You need to rest. See you in the morning at nine in the breakfast room. I will give you a mobile phone tomorrow so we can stay in touch with each other in this vast house.'

I stayed in the sitting room for another hour and heard the dogs barking somewhere outside on the property. It was the second day since the incident, and it felt like a year had passed. I went to my room and caught sight of Prue slinking her way in a red satin robe to what I imagined to be David's room. Well, each to their own. Who was I to judge? Two good souls finding comfort in each other in what I perceived to be lonely lives. Sacrificing self and serving others created loneliness. With that thought, I fell into a night of unbroken sleep until my alarm went off at 7:30 am.

Day three. Did anyone notice I was missing?

Prue was in the breakfast room, dressed in riding gear. Breakfast was laid out. Fruit, cereals, or a hot breakfast was on offer. Prue had that morning-after glow, and I hid my knowing smile.

'Good morning, I hope you slept well. We're going out riding today. Hope you like horse riding?'

'Morning, Prue, I slept like a baby. It's wonderfully quiet here. It will be good to go riding. I must ask; did you get up at the crack of dawn and prepare this amazing breakfast? It's a five-star hotel here.' I laughed and Prue glowed more.

'No, I don't cook, period! I have staff who you will never meet. My miracle workers. They slip in and do as I expect and keep to their quarters.'

'Ah. I see. Has David left?'

'Yes, we had coffee together and he's out looking at options for you.'

It was my turn to glow in knowing I knew Prue's secret without her knowing. My old schoolgirl flush returned.

We rode out after breakfast. The air was crisp and pure. Rolling hillsides overshadowed the grandness of Prue's home. Everything was large. The horse stables, the open fields and the river running through the property. How did this woman live alone in this sprawling piece of heaven? I was keen to know more about her backstory. David shared his with ease. When we stopped for a thirst break, I tried to find out whatever she was willing to share.

'Have you had more than one woman at a time seeking shelter?'

'Never, it is only one case at a time.'

'Do you ever get lonely here?'

'Why would I? I have everything I need right here. If you mean 'lonely without a partner, then that is an emphatic no! My dogs are great companions. I'll introduce you to them and you will understand why they are my best friends.'

'I'd rather not meet them. They seemed fierce when I arrived.'

'They did not have your scent then. Now notice how they react to you when you meet them. They will not harm you. You are, part of the house, to them.'

Prue's phone rang. I heard her consternation and saw her worried frown.

'That was David. He urges us to stay indoors as an apparent media report is to be broadcast at 5 pm today. Let's head back, you can meet Apollo, Mars, Mercury, and Hades.'

The Dobermans were lazing on the lawn in front of the

house. Their ears pricked up as we trotted back. They jumped to their feet to face us. This was nerve-wracking for me. I could be attacked is all I could think.

'Get off the horse, Rosa. Allow them to show you they understand who you are.'

The instant my feet touched the ground, all four Dobermans circled me. One jumped up on my chest and attempted to lick my face. The other three watched me. Prue told me to sit in a lotus position on the ground to allow for bonding. I was sniffed then licked on the arms and I reached to scratch their backs. Instantly all four turned into puppies rolling on their backs wanting more scratches.

'See why I love these fellas. They protect me and cuddle up to me.' She smiled like a content kitten.

'After what I've been through, I guess I appreciate your stance on relationships.'

'Only when you get to my age, Rosa. You have time to play the field and decide what works for you. Let's go inside. These fellas will join us in the inner courtyard.'

I was at peace this morning. How I wished it could always be like this.

THE 5 PM breaking news changed my perspective on peace. My face flashed across the television screen. The report cited Rosa Armand as armed and dangerous on the run from the law after attacking four officers from the Sigma Alpha Base.

Prue said nothing until the segment was over.

'It's a good thing we went out this morning. You must stay indoors because a massive police and army hunt will be out looking for you. The truth has been turned on its head. We must proceed with caution. David got a tip-off from an internal media source. Dirty game by these boys. Never fear we shall have them begging for mercy in a matter of days. Thankfully David had not contacted your army commander. They would have come after him.'

'I'm really sorry that this had grown to this situation.'

'Never fear, these are boys with more brawn than brain. It will unravel them. Let the fun and games begin.'

I was not so sure about fun and games. I wanted this over.

Around 11:30 pm the dogs were frantic at the front of the house. I was reading in bed and Prue was in the sitting room. There was a loud crash, I heard Prue yell, 'Fire! Fire! The alarm went off and the heavy velvet curtains were ablaze.

'Lie on the ground. Don't walk around. Someone rushed in with a hose and soon the commotion died down with the extinguished flames. We were drenched from the overactive sprinklers in the house. The distinct cry of a male voice cut through the air, 'Get this animal off me! Get it off me!'

Prue rubbed her hands together in glee.

'That must be Apollo holding the pyromaniac hostage! Stay indoors I'll go out to the firebug!'

Prue sent me a message with a photograph of the man lying on the ground. Apollo's paws pinned him down, his face a hair's breadth away from the man's neck. The image revealed the officer who pulled the gun on me at Nick's cabin.

Prue's groundsman locked the officer in a holding space next to the cellar, then she asked me to come out. The dogs turned from hunters to docile puppies the minute the intruder was apprehended.

'Are you going to call in the police?'

'Not until I have all four of them, including Nick.'

'Do you believe they will return?'

'Anything is possible, after that media manipulation.'

There was nothing else to do but wait.

DAVID CALLED Prue to say he was coming to the farm as our safety backup. Clashing with the army could be fatal for us, he warned. I knew Prue would love to have David staying at the farm. My concern was that she might drop her guard in her romantic hours and its aftermath. Prue's senses were primed for anything untoward on the property. In a short space of time, I observed her attention to detail, accuracy, and confidence in tackling anything head-on.

What I never imagined, not here, she showed me.

'We must be prepared for an advanced artillery invasion. This is why you need to know where to access our cache of arms and ammunition. She led me to the bedroom next to mine. Behind the closet was a sealed panel that even a curious or discerning eye would miss. Prue opened it with a nail file prised on the top left corner. A lone electric bulb hung on a long black cord, dead centre from the ceiling. This scene evoked a memory of the cover of *The Crucible* I had studied in junior high. A shiver tingled at the base of my neck. This hidden weaponry storehouse made me realise that Maeve, David and Prue handled challenging cases. Now my situation was classified as such. Prue handed me the nail file.

'I don't have to tell you how to use a gun, but please don't hesitate to use it. Your safety is your priority. Nobody on this property other than David or I must be trusted, understood?'

'Yes, ... I know, and it seems I am in hotter water than I first thought.'

Prue stepped out of the stash room and punched the panel back in place.

'I might move David's sleeping zone closer to you. You are the target, and we must be close at hand.'

Prue's ability to make plans, shift and reconstruct her original plan on her feet earned by profound respect. Over-thinking killed action and created lost opportunities.

Prue was the role model I had searched for my whole life.

DAVID ARRIVED AT 10 AM. He travelled through the night.

'Good morning, Rosa. Glad you both are alive to tell the tale.' He smiled and then rolled his eyes. 'Glad the perpe-trator is locked away. We must decide what we're going to do with him. He can't be held indefinitely.'

'Feed him to the dogs. Apollo would love that.'

Prue's cold suggestion shocked me. Was this just her sinister humour, or had she done that before?

'I'm going to get a few hours of sleep and then work on our next plan- of action. A clearer head is what I need.'

Prue put David in the room across the hallway from me.

My gut was uneasy. I was not free, and the threat had mounted.

Prue was busy in her study for the day. This left me to my own devices.

Lunch was served by unseen staff. I dined alone and headed back to my room. There was no sign of David yet.

I wanted to speak to my mother. She would be anxious and worried after the news flash on my apparent armed and dangerous profile warning to the public. I tried several times. There was no external line on the mobile device Prue supplied. One part of me was uneasy, and the other understood that online activities could lead my pursuers to me.

At 6 pm, Prue sent me a message saying she was dining in her room and would see me at breakfast tomorrow. I knew she was having dinner with David. I understood their need for privacy.

A restlessness consumed me. I felt confined and wanted to be outdoors. I strolled to the sitting room, poured myself a gin and tonic and headed back to my room to sleep a dead sleep to end my restlessness.

I woke up with a jolt to the sound of persistent gunfire at close range. The dogs were strangely silent during this disturbance. The gunfire stopped, and I rushed to the hidden arms room to grab a gun to protect myself. All my training as a soldier was naught if I had no weapon for self-defence.

I slipped the nail file into the left corner of the false panel. Before I could push the door open, it opened. My pulse exploded.

Prue pointed a gun at me. Her eyes were glazed. Then my hands were grabbed from behind me. David handcuffed me. No words were exchanged in those bizarre, unexpected seconds.

'Take her to my office,' Prue instructed David.

His silence scared me. The warm David I met a few days earlier, who loved the same music as I did had a sad history which he shared with ease—now mute.

Prue was in command. She circled me in the study.

'We know everything, Rosa Armand.'

It was my time to be mute.

'We know that you called your army commander from Avril's home. The persistent caller just before you and David left the house was unusual. It was your caller. Avril sent us the recording of your conversation with your commander. You caused last night's attack. We set a trap tonight to see how you would react. All I ask is, why?'

I fell to my knees, sobbing. The dam wall was down.

'I'm so sorry. It was not my intention to invite an attack. I want to remain in the army. It was my confidence-building choice. I informed my commander to assure him I had not gone AWOL, and that I was being persecuted from within Camp Alpha. I did not expect that he would turn this against me.'

'Fool!' Prue hissed.

'Confidence,' David spoke up, 'builds with life experi-ences, the pain and loss that tosses you around. That is where strength comes from. You showed cowardice. You have a lot to learn, Rosa. The first thing is to trust the right people.'

'We're done with you. David will hand you over to the local police.'

I did not protest. My poor judgement stole my chance to stand tall in my truth, be confident in my decisions, and be grateful for a helping hand.

When David led me to the van, handcuffed, the dogs, with Apollo leading the pack, growled, loping behind me.

Confidence is the ability to know when to quit trying.

I resigned myself to the notion that my challenges in life were far from over.

Also by Mala Naidoo

Novels:

Across Time and Space

Vindication Across Time

Souls of Her Daughters

Chosen Lives

What Change May Come

Aurora Days

Gallery Nights

Blackwater Mornings

Short Stories:

The Rain

Life's Seasons

Poetry:

Random Heart Poetry : Light and Shade

Random Heart Poetry : Visions and Voices

Random Heart Poetry : Time and Place

Random Heart Poetry: Rainbows and Shards

HAVE YOU READ ALL MY SHORT STORIES?

Have you read, *The Rain* and/or *Life's Seasons?*

Register for FREE short stories at www.malanaidoo.com today.

If you've enjoyed reading, *Crossings (Short Stories)* please leave an honest review on Goodreads, or any platform of your choice to help other readers decide if they might like to read my books. This will help me to write more.

With Gratitude,

Mala Naidoo

www.malanaidoo.com